P9-BIE-320

three little words

Sarah n. harvey

ORCA BOOK PUBLISHERS

Copyright © 2012 Sarah N. Harvey

All rights reserved. No part of this publication may be reproduced or transmitted
in any form or by any means, electronic or mechanical, including photocopying,
recording or by any information storage and retrieval system now known
or to be invented, without permission in writing from the publisher.

Library and Archives Canada Cataloguing in Publication

Harvey, Sarah N., 1950-
Three little words / Sarah N. Harvey.

Issued also in electronic formats.
ISBN 978-1-4598-0065-6

I. Title.
PS8615.A764T47 2012   jc813'.6   C2012-902262-4

First published in the United States, 2012
Library of Congress Control Number: 2012938211

*Orca Book Publishers is dedicated to preserving the environment and has printed
this book on paper certified by the Forest Stewardship Council®.*

Summary: When Sid leaves his foster family on their remote island home in search
of the mother he doesn't remember and a brother he's never met,
he's ill-prepared for the surprises he finds.

Orca Book Publishers gratefully acknowledges the support for its publishing
programs provided by the following agencies: the Government of Canada through
the Canada Book Fund and the Canada Council for the Arts, and the Province of British
Columbia through the BC Arts Council and the Book Publishing Tax Credit.

Cover artwork by Mike Deas
Design by Teresa Bubela
Author photo by David Lowes

ORCA BOOK PUBLISHERS   ORCA BOOK PUBLISHERS
PO Box 5626, Stn. B   PO Box 468
Victoria, BC Canada   CUSTER, WA USA
v8R 6s4   98240-0468

www.orcabook.com
Printed and bound in Canada.

15 14 13 12 • 4 3 2 1

For Robin Stevenson

Have a Heart

"Sid, this is Fariza."

Sid looks up at the sound of Megan's voice. She is standing in the kitchen doorway, her hand resting lightly on a little girl's head. The girl is wearing a long baggy gray T-shirt that stops just short of her knees. Her feet are bare and dirty; flakes of sparkly purple polish cling to her toenails. Her curly black hair is long and matted, like a feral poodle's. A beaded bracelet encircles one skinny brown wrist. She must have arrived in the night, on the last ferry. It is only seven o'clock now, barely light. Sid isn't usually up this early in the summer, but he has promised to help Caleb on the boat today, getting it ready for another charter.

"Hey," he says to the girl, "want some Cheerios?" He gestures at the yellow box on the table in front

1

of him and stands up to get another bowl from the cupboard.

The girl flinches and ducks behind Megan. Sid shrugs and goes back to his newspaper. Not that he was reading the news. He never does. He figures if something is important enough—Canada going to war, another oil spill on the coast, Brad and Angelina breaking up—he'll hear about it soon enough from his friend Chloe, who lives next door. Chloe doesn't read the newspaper either. She gets her news online: CNN, TMZ and *The New York Times*. She says news reporting is like eggs: hard-boiled, soft-boiled or medium.

No, Sid is reading the comics and grappling with the same questions he has asked ever since he was old enough to read a caption: Why is *Family Circus* still in print? Who reads it? Who likes it? Why do the kids never grow up the way they do in *For Better or Worse*? Why is everybody white? Why are their heads shaped like soccer balls? He hates *Hi and Lois* too. And *Blondie*. He imagines they all live on the same boring street in the same boring suburb. All their houses are identical and all the fathers mow their lawns on Sundays before they fire up the barbecues and char some meat. Sid smiles. Maybe the *Family Circus* mom is having an affair with Hi. Lois and Blondie become lovers and leave all the kids with the *Family Circus* grandma, whose bingo addiction gets out of control. *Family Circus* dad has a breakdown and is arrested after he robs a convenience store at gunpoint, wearing only one of his ex's aprons and high heels. Dagwood writes a tell-all memoir, gets rich and dies of a heart attack in bed with two underage male hookers dressed as Batman and Robin.

"What's so funny, Sid?" Caleb sits down at the table and reaches for the cereal.

Sid shakes his head. "Nothing. Just reading the comics."

"Did you meet our new arrival?"

"Yeah. What's up with her?"

"Emergency placement. Really bad family scene in Vancouver. She's been in care for six months, bouncing around. Social Services was looking for a long-term placement and thought she'd be better away from the city. Can't tell you much more than that."

Sid nods. Over the years he has lived with Megan and Caleb, dozens of kids have come and gone. Some stay longer than others; none has stayed as long as Sid. Fourteen years. Since he was two and Megan fished him out of the water between Megan and Caleb's boat, the *Caprice*, and the piece of shit boat he and his hippie-wannabe mom had been living on. Sid has only the wispiest memories of the boat or his birth mother. The boat—Megan says it was called *Amphitrite*, like the Greek goddess of the sea—was dark green and smelled of rotting wood and what he now knows was dope. Even now it makes him nauseous to be around anyone who's smoking up. Sid's birth mother's legal name was Deborah, but she called herself Devi, after some Hindu goddess.

The name on her son's birth certificate is Siddhartha
Eikenboom. Sid's father's name is listed as *Unknown*.

Sid was ten when Megan finally showed him his birth
certificate and explained that Siddhartha was another name
for Buddha. He was more puzzled than upset by his full
name and his birth father's anonymity. Caleb was his father,
wasn't he? Megan nodded and said she was sorry that she
didn't have any other information. Sid shrugged and asked
if he could go and play with Chloe. The birth certificate was
returned to a safe deposit box at the bank. Devi was long
gone, taking with her the knowledge of Sid's paternity—
if she ever knew it. The *Amphitrite* pulled away from the
wharf soon after Megan reported Devi to Social Services.
Devi hasn't been back nor has she stayed in touch. To Sid
she is a chimera with long red curls like his own, curls the
color of the bark of the arbutus trees that ring the cove.

Sid was Megan and Caleb's first foster child. He will
probably be their last. He can't imagine living anywhere
else. The three of them moved off the boat when Sid was
three, and there has always been another kid or two in
the big house by the ferry dock. Every time another kid
arrives, Megan says it will be the last time, but Sid knows
better. He also knows better than to get attached to any of
the other kids, especially after what happened with Tobin,
who had come to stay at the house when Sid was eleven.
Sid had thought Tobin would stay forever. Thick as thieves,
Megan always said. He really believed that they would
build a cabin in the orchard, where Sid would draw and

Tobin would play his guitar. But Tobin said he couldn't play music by himself. And an audience of one, no matter how devoted, wasn't enough. He had left six months ago, not long after he turned eighteen. He called every now and again, usually from some club, but Sid knew he wasn't coming back. Not to stay, anyway. After Tobin, Sid kept his distance from the kids who came and went.

"How old is she?" he asks now.

"Eight," Caleb replies.

"She's scared."

Caleb sighs. "Yeah. She's got reason to be. Believe me. She might be here a while."

"Cool," Sid replies. "Chloe needs a new project. She's driving me crazy."

Caleb laughs. "Good for her. That's what friends are for, right? Someone's gotta drag you away from that book." He nods toward a coil-bound sketchbook that sits on the table at Sid's elbow.

Sid spreads his hand over the book's scuffed cover, although he knows Caleb won't touch it. Respect and privacy are big in this house. Really big. Caleb is right though: left alone, Sid would sit at his desk all day, dreaming and drawing. Forgetting to eat, sleep or change his clothes, although he has a simple system for clothes. From the Ides of March to Thanksgiving he wears plain short-sleeved black T-shirts, skinny black jeans cut off to just below the knee, black Vans, no socks and a plain black ball cap. If he's cold, he puts on a plain black hoodie.

After Thanksgiving, his shirt has long sleeves, his jeans aren't cut off and he trades in his high-tops for Romeos, the slip-on boots the local fishermen wear. He wears them with thick gray woolen work socks, the kind with the red stripe at the top. The stripe is his only concession to color. He covers his curls with a Black Watch cap. He has a puffy black North Face jacket he hardly ever wears. Shopping is straightforward and relatively painless. Once in a while, on festive occasions—Christmas or his birthday—he will wear the belt Chloe bought him. Wide and black with four rows of conical studs, it makes him feel menacing, like a cop weighted down at the hips with a gun, a night stick, a Taser. When he wears it, everybody smiles, including him. He is about as menacing as a Q-tip.

Megan says he was a chatty toddler, racing up and down the wharf, investigating crab traps and coils of rope, chasing seagulls in his clunky thrift-store boots. He only believes her because he knows she doesn't lie. That child is gone. His bouncy toddler self appears only briefly in his notebook—then it is lost in the chasm between the two boats, along with one of his boots. Not that he's unhappy now—far from it—but no one would ever describe him as chatty or bouncy.

He stands up and puts his bowl in the dishwasher. "What are we doing today?" he asks Caleb.

"The usual stuff. You clean the boat and I make sure the engine's running okay. Then we'll do some grocery shopping. Hit the liquor store."

"Who's on board this time?"

"Four oil guys from Calgary. That's a lot of beer. We'll be gone by noon tomorrow. Back in a week or so, depending on the fish."

"Sounds good." Sid never goes on the charter trips with Caleb. Even if he'd felt comfortable with the kind of men who charter the boat—loud, red-faced, hearty, hard-drinking—there isn't enough room on the boat for another body, even one as skinny as Sid's. As it is, Caleb sleeps in the cockpit, under a tarp if it's raining.

Megan comes back into the kitchen as Sid is zipping up his hoodie. "I finally managed to get Fariza to sleep." She sighs. "Poor kid. I've been up with her most of the night. Maybe when she wakes up she'll feel better."

Caleb pours Megan a mug of coffee and puts it into her hands. "Sit down," he says. "I'll make you something to eat before we go."

Megan shakes her head. "I'm good. You guys get going."

"You sure?" Caleb pulls a red *Caprice Charters* ball cap over his bald head.

Megan nods. "Chloe coming over later?" she asks Sid.

He shrugs. "No doubt. Maybe she can play with the new kid."

"Maybe," Megan says, taking a sip of her coffee. "Chloe might be just what she needs."

"Chloe talks enough for two people, so you could be right," Sid says.

Caleb cuffs him good-naturedly on the shoulder and opens the back door.

"See you in a few hours," Caleb says.

"Tell Chloe I'll be back later," Sid adds.

When Sid and Caleb come back from the boat at the end of the day, Megan is in the kitchen making dinner and Chloe is in the living room, sitting cross-legged on one end of the couch. Fariza is at the other end. A mountain of stuffed animals sits between them. Bears, zebras, cats, dogs, wolves, whales, deer, mice, parrots, giraffes, rabbits, monkeys, cows, penguins, moose, lambs, raccoons, foxes, owls, dolphins. Megan has been collecting them for years. Each new kid gets to choose and keep one. Sid still has the porcupine he chose when he was two; he named it Spike. Not very original, he thinks now, but Spike still sits on Sid's windowsill, his quills gathering dust. Fariza is clutching a gigantic pink flamingo by its scrawny neck. She is dressed in clothes that Sid recognizes from helping with the laundry. Stuffed animals are not the only things Megan collects. There is a cupboard full of used clothing upstairs, all sizes and styles. Everything from flip-flops to parkas. You could outfit a whole village in Africa from that cupboard.

Fariza has chosen an oversize red T-shirt, baggy cargo shorts and neon-green Crocs. From the first day, kids are allowed to choose their own clothes. Megan says it makes them feel more in control. Sid vaguely remembers loving a hand-knit red sweater with a spaceship on the back, and he still pays attention to what kids choose out of the clothes cupboard. Looking at Fariza, he thinks how much she looks like a little boy in an older brother's hand-me-downs. Most of the girls who come to stay at the house gravitate toward skirts and shirts that are too tight and too short. They paw through the clothes cupboard, pouncing on bright colors and anything that sparkles. When Tobin first arrived, he traded his Walmart jeans for a men's kilt, which he wore with an assortment of wrinkled plaid shirts. Sid waited for him to get beat up, or at least bullied, but it never happened. Not to his knowledge anyway. He figured it helped that at fifteen, Tobin was six foot six and tattooed like a Samoan warrior.

"You and Fariza waiting for an ark, Chloe?" Caleb says as he and Sid shuck off their shoes by the front door.

"Might as well be," Chloe says. "Megan said it was okay to get out the stuffies. I thought maybe it would make Fariza feel better. I tried reading to her, but she won't sit close enough to me to see the pictures. Which means I couldn't do her hair or nails either." Chloe jumps up, causing an avalanche of animals. Fariza cringes deeper into the cushions.

Sid looks down at the pile of books on the battered wooden coffee table. All his old favorites: *Where the Wild Things Are, Peepo, Mr. Gumpy's Outing, Blueberries for Sal.* After Megan rescued him, all he wanted to do was sit beside her on the old green corduroy couch and trace his fingers over the pictures as she read. Over the years he has read to his share of kids. Some frightened, some angry, some inconsolable. Some of them couldn't sit still for very long, some of them fell asleep while he was reading, some of them sucked their thumbs, some of them smacked the books with an open palm or sucked on the corners. No matter what they did, Sid just kept reading. *Mr. Gumpy owned a boat and his house was by a river.* He wants to tell Chloe that she should be more patient, but she's already pulling on her shoes, babbling about being late for dinner, and how Irena, her grandmother, will kill her if she doesn't set the table. Patience is not Chloe's strength. Sid looks over at Caleb, who raises his eyebrows.

"Irena runs a tight ship," Caleb agrees. Chloe's grandmother is a legendary island matriarch: stern, demanding but also, in Sid's experience, intelligent, kind (to him anyway) and an awesome cook.

"Everything okay out here?" Megan says from the kitchen doorway. Her round face is flushed and sweaty, her khaki shorts wrinkled, her T-shirt stained. She wipes her hands on her shorts, leaving a trail of flour. "What did I miss?"

"Nothing," Caleb says. "Just Chloe racing off like she's got a bee in her bra."

Sid snorts. Chloe blushes and glares at him.

"It's been a long day," Megan says. "Chloe, I'd never have gotten my work done without you. Are you sure you won't stay for dinner?"

Chloe shakes her head. "No thanks, Megan. I told Mom I'd be back."

Sid squats down in front of Fariza and peers into her eyes, which he expects to be brown. Instead, they are as green as a stick of celery. She turns away and buries her face in a panda bear's belly, but she seems more shy than frightened now.

"She won't talk, you know," Chloe says. "All she says is please and thank you."

"I know," Sid replies. "I don't mind. Kind of a nice change. She can talk or not. Doesn't matter to me." He straightens up and pats the flamingo's head.

Chloe slams the door on her way out.

"What's that about?" Sid says to no one in particular. He's used to Chloe's emotional storms—they've been friends forever—but lately she often seems on edge or angry or upset. He wants to ask why, but he knows better than to ask a question when he's afraid of the answer. He has learned the hard way that nothing stays the same, no matter how much he wants it to.

"Women," Caleb says.

"What's that supposed to mean?" Megan asks.

"Nothing." Caleb laughs and puts his arm around Megan. "Can't live without 'em."

"You got that right," she says. "Sid, wash your hands and then set the table, please. Maybe Fariza could help you."

Sid nods. Another one of Megan's theories is that helping out around the house makes kids feel better.

Sid's specialty is laundry. Collecting it, sorting it, folding it, putting it away. He hates ironing though. Not a good job for a daydreamer, Caleb said after Sid burnt a hole in one of Caleb's good shirts.

"Yo, Fariza," Sid says. "You wanna wash up first?"

Fariza blinks her huge green eyes and then slides off the couch and scurries past him, dragging the flamingo behind her. When he comes into the kitchen, she is hiding behind Megan, shifting the flamingo from hand to hand.

"She's had some bad experiences with boys," Megan says.

Who hasn't? Sid thinks as he gets the cutlery out of the drawer. Chloe and her girlfriends are always talking about how lame guys are, and he stills feel the sting of Tobin's absence. He circles the table—knife, fork, spoon; knife, fork, spoon. Cloth napkins folded in triangles to the left of each fork. Water glasses at the tips of the knives. Fariza has come out from behind Megan. He can feel her watching him as he moves around the table. He puts a hot-pink napkin at one place, and a glass painted with the Little Mermaid.

He points and says, "That's your place, Fariza. And here's a chair for your friend." He pulls up an extra chair, and Fariza seats the flamingo on it. Its head flops forward onto the table, like a guest who's had too much to drink. "Thank you," Fariza whispers.

"You're welcome," Sid replies, bowing slightly.

It's All Good

Caleb says that Sid's the only teenager on the planet who doesn't look on summer vacation as an opportunity to sleep all day, stay up all night and spend as much waking time as possible away from adults. Sid knows he is lucky not to have to find a summer job. Caleb pays him to help out on the boat, and since Sid's material needs are minimal—art supplies and the occasional movie and burger in town—he is able to spend his days doing the things he loves: drawing, riding his bike around the island, swimming with Chloe in Merriweather Lake, which is a half-hour bike ride from his house. He and Chloe have a lake ritual: they race back and forth across the lake (Sid always wins), they have a handstand contest in the shallows (Chloe always wins) and then they lie on the sun-warmed rocks and eat salt-and-vinegar chips and talk.

Mostly Chloe talks and Sid listens. After a morning spent drawing, Sid welcomes Chloe's chatter. Without her, he would probably sink even further into the world he has created on the page. A world he has been inhabiting since Megan first sat him down at the scarred kitchen table and gave him crayons and a piece of paper.

Now, every day after breakfast (Cheerios on weekdays, scrambled eggs on Saturdays, waffles on Sundays), he takes his place at the table, his pens and pencils laid out neatly in front of him, his sketchbook open. Before he begins to draw, he always gazes out the window at the cove, noting which fish boats are at the government wharf, how many cars are lined up for the next ferry, whether the eagle, which he long ago named Eric, is in its nest at the top of the fir tree near the dock. Only when he has scanned the view, does he start to draw. He knows he's a bit OCD—he even read a book about it to make sure he's not completely crazy—but he's not an obsessive hand-washer or anything. His routines don't hurt anybody. He has learned to be flexible when he has to be. He knows Megan and Caleb worry about it, but he figures it's better than worrying about whether he's doing drugs or fighting in the ferry parking lot after too many beers. Lots of their foster kids have been way more trouble than he is.

Today, a week after her arrival, Fariza is sitting beside him at the table, her flamingo in her lap and the remains of her Cheerios in front of her. She and Sid had named the flamingo one rainy afternoon. Sid came up with name after name—Frank, Fritz, Fanny, Frieda, Ferdinand, Fitzroy, Finn, Freya, Francine. None of them got a nod from Fariza. He tried again—Flora, Floyd, Frodo, Fiona, Fred. When he said *Fred*, Fariza nodded and smiled.

"Hey, Fred," Sid says now. "How's it going?"

Fred, of course, is silent, as is Fariza.

"Good Cheerios?" Sid says to Fariza.

She nods.

"I'm gonna draw now, Fariza. We'll read later, okay?"

Fariza nods again, clears her bowl from the table and sits down next to Sid again after making Fred comfortable on the couch. She points at Sid's sketchbook, which is open to a fresh page.

"What?" he asks. "You want to seé it?"

Fariza nods and turns the pages back to the beginning of the sketchbook.

Sid has never shown his work to anyone but Tobin, whose one-word comment was "Disturbing." He suspects that Chloe—and lots of the foster kids over the years—would sneak a peek if he left the book lying around, so the sketchbook is either with him or locked in a cedar trunk in his room with the dozens of other black hardcover sketchbooks he has filled over the years. Always the same brand as the first one Megan bought him. Always the same size. Always coil-bound. The key to the trunk lives on a silver chain around his neck.

Sid inhales deeply as Fariza strokes the first page of the book. What could be the harm in showing her? he thinks.

It's not like she's going to talk about it. And it's not really that disturbing. At least he doesn't think so. He had been hurt by Tobin's comment—more hurt than he ever let on.

"So, I started this story about a year ago. It's about a village called Titan Arum, in a place called the Uncanny Valley." He clears his throat. Talking about it is hard— harder than drawing it, almost. "Titan Arum is named after a huge plant that grows in the valley. The flower can be as much as nine feet tall. Way taller than Caleb. And it smells really, really bad, like a super-stinky fart," he says. Fariza places her hand over her mouth and giggles. The sound is almost shocking, as if a kitten had barked. "But there's only one person in the whole village who can smell it and that's him." Sid points to a small skinny figure dressed in a striped T-shirt and baggy shorts. "He's the main character. His name is Billy. No one believes that the big flower smells, so the townspeople think he's crazy." He stops again, not wanting to tell her about how badly Billy is treated, how hungry he is, how alone. He doesn't tell her that Billy is the only character who never has a speech balloon above his head. He figures Fariza doesn't need any more encouragement not to speak.

"Anyway, so the book is about Billy's, uh, adventures in the Uncanny Valley." He flips forward quickly to a blank page and tears it out of the book. Fariza watches as he neatly sections the page in half—two rectangles, one on top of the other—and sets it in front of her.

"Colored pencils or felt pens?" he asks. "Take your pick. Or I can get you some crayons."

Fariza stares at the paper, but she doesn't move to pick up a pen or pencil.

"Want me to start you off?" Sid asks. Fariza nods and watches as he picks up a black pen and draws in the top box. A small female figure with curly hair materializes on the page, sitting on an oversize couch. Next to her is a smiling flamingo, all gangly neck and crossed spindly legs. Above Fred's head is the puffy cloud of a speech balloon. Sid uses felt pens to color the girl's skin brown, her T-shirt red, the flamingo pink, the couch green. At the top of the page, he prints *The Amazing Adventures of Fariza and Fred.* His printing is small and precise, like something you'd see on a blueprint. He slides the paper back to Fariza, who smiles and picks up a pencil.

Every morning after the breakfast dishes are done and before they sit down to draw, Fariza helps Sid sort the dirty laundry, solemnly dropping the whites in one pile, the colors in another, after carefully reading the washing instructions on the labels. The whole process slows to a crawl as she searches for labels on ancient shorts and threadbare shirts, but Sid never rushes her. He folds clean towels while she works. Cleans the lint trap on the dryer. Pairs up socks. She reads well for an eight-year-old, he thinks as she holds up a silky blouse of Megan's and points at the label. *Dry Clean Only*, it says. She shakes her head and puts the blouse to one side.

"Good call," Sid says. Fariza nods and keeps sorting, frowning when she can find no label. Even without a label, though, she knows what to do.

"She's done that before," Sid says to Megan one morning as he and Fariza arrange their pens and pencils on the table.

"Done what?" Megan asks. She is sitting on the green couch reading a cookbook, her half-glasses perched on the end of her nose.

"Laundry."

"I wouldn't be surprised," Megan replies.

Megan makes a rule of never telling Sid the histories of the kids who come to live with them. *If they want to tell you, they can,* she always says. *They're not my stories to tell. And besides, it's best to draw conclusions about people from your own experience of them, not from a case history some overworked social worker wrote after a long hard day.* Not that Megan has anything against social workers—she was one for many years—she just wants Sid to get to know the kids on his, and their, own terms. She doesn't knowingly take in violent kids or kids with drug and alcohol problems, although many of her charges come from homes where violence and substance abuse are the norm. Some kids want to talk about what has brought them to the island; others don't. No one ever pushed Sid to talk, and he isn't usually inclined to pry.

Even though Sid knows Megan probably won't tell him, there's something about Fariza—her silence, probably—that makes him want to find out what happened to her. If he ever does ask Megan about it though, it won't be with Fariza in the room. He'll have to be careful. Her silence makes it so easy to forget she's there.

All he says now is, "She reads really well."

Megan looks up from her cookbook. "Really? How can you tell?"

"She reads the washing instructions on the labels when we do the laundry. Never gets it wrong. She kept that yellow silk blouse of yours out of the hot wash a few days ago."

"That's great, Fariza," Megan says. "Thank you, sweetie. I love that blouse."

Fariza and Sid take their places, side by side, at the table. Side by side, they stare out at the cove for a few minutes. Fariza points at the top of the fir tree and then flaps her arms.

"Yup, there's Eric," Sid says. He points at a green car in the ferry lineup. "It looks like Chloe and her mom are going to town."

"The party's this weekend," Megan says. "I'm trying to find a new dessert to make."

"What—no éclairs?" Sid gasps and puts his hand to his heart. "Megan's éclairs are awesome," he says to Fariza, who is looking both puzzled and worried. "Whipped cream and chocolate sauce. Mmmmm.

Midsummer Madness without éclairs? No way. Next you're gonna tell me that Irena's not making her famous potato salad or Caleb isn't barbecuing salmon."

"He's such a traditionalist," Megan says to Fariza, who still looks puzzled.

"Someone who hates change," Megan explains. "If you want éclairs, you're going to have to make them yourself, Sid. Last year I made three dozen. I'd be happy to pass the torch to you. You up for it?"

Sid nods. "Me and Fariza will do it. Right, Fariza?"

Fariza nods.

"You don't know what you've signed up for." Megan laughs. "I'll get the groceries today. The party's in three days. Don't leave it till the last minute."

"No worries," Sid says. "I've been helping you since I was four. I think I can whip up a few dozen éclairs—no problem."

He sits down beside Fariza and opens his sketchbook. Every day he tears out a page, divides it into boxes and draws something in the upper half. Every day, Fariza fills in Fred's speech balloon and writes some more of the story in the bottom box. The next day, Sid draws what she has written the previous day. Right now, cartoon Fariza and cartoon Fred are about to embark on a kayak trip. Fred is having a hard time getting into the kayak. *My legs are too long*, it says in his speech balloon. *And I don't have any arms. You'll have to paddle.* Sid draws the scene and then hands the page back to Fariza, who immediately starts to write in the lower box. Her printing is smaller and neater than it was when they first started working together; she fills the space below the drawing with line after line of words, her fingers clutching the pencil fiercely. She is already developing a bump on her middle finger, just like Sid's.

As she writes, Sid considers Billy's ordeal in the Uncanny Valley. For the first time since he began the story, he wonders whether he wants to continue with it. Nothing good ever happens to Billy; maybe he should just wander into the forest of Titan Arum and be poisoned by the stench. When his body is finally found, his family will realize that he was right all along—the giant plants are indeed toxic—and they will set up a memorial in his memory. End of story. Sid closes the sketchbook. He has never felt this way about one of his creations. Never wanted to kill off a character. He looks over at Fariza, whose tongue is protruding as she fills another line with tiny print.

"I'll be back in a minute," he says to her. She nods slightly but doesn't raise her eyes from the paper.

Sid goes up to his room and takes a brand-new coil-bound sketchbook from a stack on his bookcase. He goes back to Fariza, and waits for her to finish writing. While he waits, he opens the new sketchbook and writes *The Amazing Adventures of Fariza and Fred* at the top of the first page. Underneath he writes *Written by Fariza and Illustrated by Sid*. Under that, he draws Fariza and

Fred on the couch. Then he takes the half-dozen pages they have already completed and carefully tapes them into the book. When Fariza finally puts down her pencil, he hands her the sketchbook.

"You and Fred need your own book," he says. "Just like mine."

Fariza's eyes widen as she opens the book and sees her name on the page.

"Thank you," she whispers. Her voice is scratchy but sweet. She pats his hand before picking up the book and hugging it to her chest. She slides off the chair and goes over to the couch, where Fred is waiting for her.

Laugh Out Loud

"I bet you wish Tobin was here," Chloe says.

Sid shrugs. "Yeah. I guess." He knows better than to tell Chloe how much he misses Tobin. Chloe had a crush on Tobin, but Tobin wasn't interested. It's not a topic he and Chloe discuss.

"Remember the time you and Tobin took off in Nancy Benton's Porsche?" Chloe says. "Irena was so pissed."

Sid grins. Two summers ago, at Midsummer Madness, he and Tobin had been doing what he and Chloe are doing today: directing guests to parking spots in the field beside Chloe's house. Irena has thrown an August long-weekend potluck open house for over thirty years—all permanent residents of the island (and their families) are welcome. No summer visitors (triflers, Irena calls them) permitted. Since Irena knows each and every person who lives year-round on the island, it is impossible to crash the party, although many have tried. Nancy Benton's parents still live one cove over, so Nancy's presence is acceptable. More than acceptable—she is a celebrity, an island girl who made good in Hollywood.

"Nancy didn't mind," Sid says. "In fact, she asked Tobin if he wanted to take it for a spin. Said every boy should have a chance to drive a car like that. He'd just got his Learner's permit. Remember? Irena wasn't the only one who was pissed. I seem to recall you refusing to come out of your room."

Chloe snorted. "That wasn't because of you, asshole. It was because Irena was treating me like her personal slave. *Chloe, get more chairs. Chloe, the silverware isn't shiny enough. Chloe, you can't wear that. Chloe, your hair is a disgrace.* And anyway, Nancy Benton is so full of herself, now that she's finally in a hit series. Mom says everyone's conveniently forgotten what a bitch she was in high school."

Sid raises an eyebrow at her. "Since when do you care? Anyway, she seems nice enough to me. Maybe she'll turn up again this year—in a Ferrari. You telling me you wouldn't want to go for a spin?"

Chloe swats him on the arm as a perfectly maintained baby-blue Studebaker parks in the circular driveway. An elderly gentleman in a beautiful cream-colored suit and matching fedora emerges slowly from the car and hands Sid the keys.

"Be careful with her," he says to Sid as Chloe takes his arm and helps him up the front stairs.

"Always, Mr. Goodwyn," Sid says. "You'll get the primo spot near the front door."

The guests begin to arrive in a steady stream—on foot, by bicycle, in battered old cars and shiny new trucks. Some even come by kayak or canoe and walk up from the cove. Some bear armloads of flowers; one little girl has a daisy chain she has made for Chloe. Others carry casserole dishes full of hot wings, paper plates piled with Nanaimo Bars, Tupperware containers full of three-bean salad. And then there are the chips—bags and bags of chips in every variety and flavor imaginable. Sid knows how Irena feels about chips—she calls bringing chips and dips to a potluck *the ultimate social sin*—but after he's been on parking duty for an hour, he's ready to rip into the next bag of chips he sees.

Megan appears on the front porch with Fariza, who holds a can of Coke in each hand. Fariza's hair is in neat cornrows, punctuated at the tips by tiny glass beads. Chloe's mission, since Fariza's arrival on the island, has been to tame Fariza's wild hair. She started her campaign slowly, showing Fariza pictures she found online, explaining how she would get the tangles out first, using lots of conditioner so it wouldn't hurt. But it was the seaglass beads—soft blues and greens, milky white—that finally won Fariza over. Chloe's mom had found them at a local craft fair years before and kept them in an old Mason jar on the kitchen windowsill. Chloe loved to play with the beads, running them through her hands like water. Now the beads click whenever Fariza turns her head. When she is anxious or tired, she strokes one particular green bead—the color of her eyes—that dangles near her chin.

"We thought you might need a break," Megan says. Fariza solemnly hands Sid and Chloe the drinks. "Go inside and get something to eat. Fariza and I will take over out here."

"Are you sure?" Sid says.

Megan nods. "You don't want to miss Irena's potato salad, do you?"

"Nope," Sid says. "And I better snag a few éclairs before they're all gone. Did you get one, Fariza?" They had spent the day before in the kitchen—beating the glossy batter, melting the dark chocolate—and this morning cutting open the éclairs and stuffing the cavities with whipped cream.

Fariza nods and rubs her belly.

As usual there are more people than chairs, so Sid helps Caleb drag furniture from the house out onto the lawn—dining-room chairs, footstools, the wicker settee off the front porch, an old office chair, even the coffee table is pressed into service. Blankets are thrown on the lawn; only a narrow path is left down the broad front stairs. People begin to trail out of the house, balancing plastic wineglasses and plates piled precariously high with food.

Blankets become tablecloths for impromptu picnics; chairs are pulled into circles around invisible tables. Conversations become more animated as the wine and beer flow and the food and the weather work their usual magic. The mouse-squeaks of plastic cutlery on Styrofoam plates are drowned out by shouts of laughter and the siren wail of a tired baby. Someone has put an old James Taylor CD on the stereo.

> I've seen fire and I've seen rain
> Sunny days that I thought would never end
> I've seen lonely times when I could not find a friend
> But I always thought that I'd see you again.

Why are they playing such a sad song? Sid wonders. Every single person here—well, anyone over the age of ten anyway—must have someone they miss, someone they shared endless sunny days with, someone who has disappeared out of their lives. But no one else seems to notice or care. Not Chloe, who has never known her father. Not Irena, whose husband died years ago. Not Megan and Caleb, who may have wanted children of their own, not just other people's damaged cast-offs. They all seem so happy—carefree even. Even Irena, who is often gruff and imperious, loves her island life. Loves chopping wood, growing raspberries, ordering her family around.

Someone turns off the stereo, and now guitars are coming out of cases, bongo drums are clasped between bare knees. Someone has brought a banjo; two little girls tune tiny violins. Small hands reach into a basket full of child-size instruments: tambourines, triangles, maracas. Sid grabs two kazoos and goes to find Fariza. Chloe is with some of her friends from school, shrieking and giggling near where Craig Benton, Nancy's nephew, is lying, shirtless, on a wicker lounger, a beer in one hand, a cigarette in the other. Craig is a douche, in Sid's opinion, a good-looking loser with no ambition and fewer brains. He got his last girlfriend pregnant. She quit school to raise his kid. Sid can't stand to watch Chloe with him.

He finds Fariza curled up with Fred in the window seat that overlooks the front lawn and the sea. It's one of his favorite spots in the house, one he always comes to when he visits Chloe and she starts to get on his nerves. The blue-and-white-striped cushions are worn but clean, and there is a quilt for when it cools down. There's always something to see: a tugboat towing a ridiculously long log boom, the ferry chugging back and forth to the big island, seagulls arguing over dead fish, a luxury yacht flying an American flag, a sailboat with rainbow sails, a pod of killer whales. Today there are eight fish boats heading north. Fariza points and holds up eight fingers and then points to herself.

"Eight, right," Sid says. "I brought you something." He hands her a red plastic kazoo.

Fariza takes it and turns it over and over in her hands but doesn't bring it to her lips. It's obvious she has no idea what to do with it.

Sid sits down beside her on the window seat. "You know that song 'The Wheels on the Bus'?" he asks. He has heard Megan singing the old familiar songs to Fariza in the middle of the night, coaxing her back to sleep after a nightmare.

Fariza nods.

"Can you hum it for me?"

Fariza nods again and starts to hum.

Sid brings a green kazoo to his lips and starts to hum too. Fariza squeals and does the same. After "The Wheels on the Bus," they hum "Down By the Bay," "Frère Jacques," "I'm a Little Teapot," "Baby Beluga" and "London Bridge." Fariza doesn't seem to know "Puff the Magic Dragon" or "Rubber Ducky," but she claps for Sid when he hums them. When they run out of kids' songs, they sit and listen to the music that wafts through the open windows. When Sid hears a song he likes, he hums along on the kazoo—"Hey Jude," "The Night They Drove Old Dixie Down," "Scarborough Fair"—but when someone starts to sing "Bad Moon Rising," he puts the kazoo down and listens: *I see a bad moon risin' / I see trouble on the way / I see earthquakes and lightnin' / I see bad times today.* Fariza watches him, one hand on Fred, the other clutching the kazoo. When her eyelids start to droop, Sid covers her and

Fred with the quilt and sits with her as the sun goes down. A solitary guitarist sings, "*Good night, Irene, good night, Irene / I'll see you in my dreams*" as the guests start to drift away and the moon rises over the sea.

The morning after the party, Fariza and Megan sleep in.

"Too much partying," Caleb says when Sid asks where they are. "Fariza had a bad night. Megan had a hard time calming her down. None of the usual stuff worked. They finally got to sleep as the sun came up."

Sid feels guilty—maybe it was a bad idea to let her listen to "Bad Moon Rising." She sure didn't need to worry about any more trouble finding her. He's about to ask Caleb what brought Fariza to the island, when he hears Chloe's voice coming from the downstairs bathroom. Suddenly he remembers that they had made plans to go to the lake today. Start early and spend the day there. He hasn't felt like drawing lately and he hasn't been to the lake since Fariza arrived. He needs a day off.

The song Chloe is singing is not one he knows. Her taste in music had shifted recently, from angry indie bands to something he can only describe as girly. Her iPod is full of stuff he doesn't recognize.

"You're a musical dinosaur," she had told him recently.

"Fine by me," he replied. "I always wanted to be a velociraptor."

"More like a diplodocus," she said. "You know—
a big dumb vegetarian who likes the Beatles and James
Taylor and Simon and Garfunkel."

He goes upstairs to his room and changes into some
blue board shorts he bought for two bucks at a yard sale.
He drapes a threadbare Batman towel over his T-shirt like
a cape and goes back downstairs. No Chloe.

"You ready yet?" Sid bangs on the bathroom door.

"Chill out." Chloe's voice is muffled. "The lake's not
going anywhere."

"But the sun is," Sid mutters as he puts water bottles
and power bars in his pack and then slips on his Vans.

Lately Chloe has been spending a lot of time fussing
with her hair, checking her eye makeup, applying lip
gloss every five minutes, it seems. Their trips to the lake
used to involve five minutes of preparation: bathing
suits under shorts and T-shirts, towels, sunscreen, water,
snacks. Stuff everything in a backpack. Jump on their
bikes. Things are different now. Not bad; just different.

When Chloe finally emerges from the bathroom,
she is wearing the smallest bikini Sid has ever seen.
He looks away, startled by the sight of Chloe's breasts,
which are barely contained by tiny triangles of what
looks like the crocheting Megan sometimes does on
winter nights. Chloe has clearly gotten over her childhood hatred of her body. She still calls herself the
Polish Peasant—she's short and strong, with a round
face, brown eyes and thick dark hair—but she laughs

now when she says it. She calls her mother and grand-mother the Polish Princesses: high cheekbones, long legs, full lips, straight blond tresses. When she turned thir-teen, Chloe got something her mother and grandmother didn't have: big breasts and a high round butt. Or, as she calls them, B&B: boobs and booty. Almost overnight, she shed her oversize T-shirts and baggy sweats in favor of mini-skirts and tank tops, but Sid has never seen her in anything as revealing as the bikini she has on now. It occurs to him that over the years, Chloe's bathing suits have gotten smaller and his have gotten bigger. Right now he's grateful for his baggy board shorts.

"You like?" Chloe twirls around as if she's in a ball gown. Her butt is bursting out of another microscopic cobweb of material. Caleb coughs and goes to the kitchen.

"Uh, sure," Sid says. "Don't you want to put on a T-shirt or something though?" He can't see how it would be comfortable to ride for half an hour over the bumpy island roads clad only in what is essentially a sexy doily collection.

Chloe laughs. "That's why I have this," she says, slip-ping on a sheer flowered tunic that barely covers her butt. "I got it on eBay. Isn't it awesome? It's Tory Burch."

"Tory Burch. Wow." Sid has no idea who Tory Burch is, but he knows he's supposed to be impressed. "Those too?" he asks, pointing to Chloe's feet. Her flip-flops have big pink flowers between the toes.

"No, silly. Old Navy," Chloe replies. "Five bucks. And yeah, I know—not good for a long bike ride. I brought these." She holds up an ancient pair of Tevas. "I'm not a complete idiot, you know."

"Never said you were," Sid replies as they head out the door to their bikes.

Hear Me Out

When Sid and Chloe return at the end of the day, hungry and sunburned, a car Sid has never seen is in the driveway. It's an ancient red Ford Woodie in mint condition, with the words *Windfall Woodworking by Phileas Phine* painted in curving white script on the side. What kind of people name a kid Phileas? Sid wonders as he puts his bike in the shed.

"Awesome car," Chloe says when he comes out.

"Probably another kid," Sid says, although he can't imagine why someone with a car like that would be delivering a child to Megan. Usually social workers drive drab, dusty sedans—silver or beige. "You coming in?" he asks Chloe.

"Nope," she says, hopping back on her bike. "Gotta shower. My hair's a disaster. Me and some of the girls are going to town tonight. Craig's driving. Wanna come?"

"I don't think so," Sid says. "Thanks for asking though." He can think of nothing he'd enjoy less than a night in town with that asshole Craig and a bunch of giggling girls. Chloe's girlfriends are okay, but he can never think of anything to say to them. He doesn't watch the same movies or listen to the same music. He doesn't own a cell phone—service on the island is spotty at best—or have high-speed Internet access.

"Call me," Chloe yells over her shoulder as she rides off.

Sid climbs the steps to the front porch and pauses with his hand on the worn brass doorknob. After a day in the sun with Chloe, all he wants is quiet and solitude, but if there's a guest in the house or a new kid, he's going to have to suck it up. Megan raised him to be polite. *You don't have to say much*, she told him over and over when he was growing up. *But you do have to be polite.* A firm handshake is good, mumbling and staring at the floor is bad. Ignoring people is the worst. Maybe today he'll be able to get away with a quick hello and a dash up the stairs to the shower.

As soon as he opens the door, he has a feeling he's not going to get his shower anytime soon.

"Sid?" Megan's voice comes from what used to be the dining room, and is now what Caleb calls Megan's War Room and Spa. Part office, part craft room, part retreat. If Megan is in there with the door shut, she is not to be disturbed unless the house is on fire. Usually the door is open, as it is now.

"We're in here, honey," she calls. *Honey?* Definitely something going on. Megan hasn't called him honey since he was six.

When he walks into the dining room, everyone stands up, as if he is a visiting dignitary. There are only three people in the room—Megan, Caleb and a middle-aged man who is now moving toward Sid with his hand outstretched.

Sid shakes the man's hand—firmly, but not too firmly, as Caleb has taught him—and steps back. "Where's Fariza?" he asks.

"Napping," Megan says. "She had a bad day. Sid, this is Phil. He's come up from Victoria to see you."

"Me?"

Megan nods.

"Why?" Sid turns back to Phil. "I don't know you, do I?" He looks at the man more closely, searching for something familiar. Phil is short—maybe five foot five—and muscular. He's wearing a tight white T-shirt and soft loose jeans, the kind with a loop to hang a hammer. He is completely bald. Sid suppresses a laugh. Phil looks like Mr. Clean, if Mr. Clean had been put in a hot dryer.

Phil clears his throat, and Sid realizes the man is nervous. More accurately, Sid is making the man nervous. This happens rarely enough that Sid almost enjoys it, although he feels kind of sorry for the guy too.

"Phil has something to tell you, Sid," Caleb says. "Why don't we all sit down?"

"I'll get some tea," Megan says, rushing out of the room.

Now it's Sid's turn to be nervous. He sits on the edge of one of the dining-room chairs, suddenly aware that his board shorts are still damp. He can't imagine what this stranger wants to tell him. Well, that's not exactly true. He *can* imagine it. He's been imagining it—and dreading it—for fourteen years. His very own Darth Vader moment. A strange man turns up and says, "Sid, I am your father." But surely there would be something— even something small, like an unnaturally long big toe or a crooked incisor—that Sid would recognize. He glances down at Phil's beat-up Nikes. No help there. And Phil isn't smiling as he sits down opposite Sid and clears his throat again.

"It's beautiful up here," he says. Sid nods. "Great place to grow up, eh?"

Sid nods again. Sweat has started to bead up under his hairline and trickle down his back. He itches to jump in the shower and stay there until this midget disappears. Megan comes back into the room with a tray full of tea things. Phil dumps some milk into his tea; Sid takes a swig from his water bottle.

"Do you remember your mother?" Phil asks.

Sid shakes his head. "Not really. Just her hair."

"Her hair was beautiful," Phil says.

"Was?"

"She shaved it off a few years ago, when she started to go gray."

"Oh."

"Not very talkative, are you, son?" Phil says.

"Nope. And I'm not your son. Caleb's my dad."

Phil puts down his mug and sits back in his chair. He exhales forcefully, like one of the sea lions on the rocks in the cove. A very small sea lion.

"No, you're not my son. And I know Caleb is your dad. I'm a friend of your mother's, of Devorah's."

"Did she send you?" Sid croaks, his mouth suddenly dry.

"No. I don't know where she is."

"Then why are you here?"

"I thought she might have come here. Looking for you."

"Why now?"

Phil shrugs. "She went off her meds, started talking about you a lot. Then she took off. But Megan and Caleb are pretty sure she's not here."

So go away, Sid thinks. Leave us alone. But part of him wants to know what this man can tell him. Needs to know, in fact.

Megan reaches out and rubs his shoulder. "I know this is a lot to take in, Sid. Why don't you go and have a shower, take a little time. Phil's going to stay the night. We'll have lots of time to talk."

He smiles at her gratefully and leaves the room.

When he comes down an hour later, Megan is in the kitchen with Fariza, who is standing on a stool, licking cake batter off a spatula. Caleb and Phil are nowhere to be seen.

"I sent them to the store to get some ice cream for the cake Fariza and I made," Megan says. "Figured we could talk a bit before they came back."

"Okay." Sid leans his back against the counter by the sink. "What did you want to talk about?"

"Are you ready to hear about your mother?"

"I don't know. I guess so." Sid watches Megan's face, hoping for some clue, something that will help him figure out what to feel. Besides confused and frightened and a bit angry.

"It sounds like she's had a lot of problems. Mental health problems," Megan says.

"You mean she's nuts. That would explain a lot." Sid sounds bitter, even to his own ears.

"Well, it would, actually," Megan says. "Phil says she was diagnosed as bipolar years ago, but she'd probably been sick a long time. Certainly since before you were born. She's been better since she's been taking meds, more stable."

"Until now."

Megan nods.

"And he thinks she'll come looking for me," Sid says.

Megan nods again. "Maybe. But there's something else."

"What?"

"She had another child thirteen years ago. Another boy. His name is Gawain. She left him on his own when she disappeared. And now he's gone too. Phil is very worried—about both of them."

Sid turns to look out the open window over the sink. There is a hummingbird at the feeder, and he can smell the sweet peas Megan always plants right below the window. "I have a brother," he says without turning around.

"A half brother, yes," Megan says.

"A missing half brother. No father. And a crazy mother. Great."

Fariza hops off her stool and drags it over next to Sid at the sink. She climbs up beside him and reaches up to pat his cheek. She starts to hum "The Farmer in the Dell," and Sid smiles faintly and hums along.

At dinner, Phil seems reluctant to talk about Sid's mother and half brother. Maybe it's Fariza's silent presence; maybe it's Sid's refusal to broach the subject. At any rate, they talk about other things: fish farms, deforestation, the latest round of government cuts to social services. Phil talks about his passion for exotic wood. He only works with wood from windfalls, and he talks about wood the way other men talk about luxury cars or women. He tells them his car's name is Miss Havisham, after a character in a Dickens novel. Turns out Phil is a Dickens freak: his cats are named Dodger, Fagin and Smike.

"You got any pets, Sid?" he asks.

Sid shakes his head. "Allergic."

"Like your mother," Phil says. "She always wanted a cat, but they make her sneeze."

"And she probably would have forgotten to feed it," Sid mutters. It comes out meaner than he meant it to.

Phil stares at him, as if seeing him for the first time. After a long moment, he says, "Do you want to know about her, or have you already decided to hate her?" When Sid doesn't respond, Phil gets up from the table and starts clearing the dishes.

Megan glares at Sid. "Phil, please sit down. Sid, there's no need to be rude. I know this is hard, but I think you should listen to Phil. Fariza and I are going to clear up the dishes. You men can sit on the porch and talk—or not."

"Sorry," Sid mumbles, more to Megan than to Phil. He hates disappointing her. But what more does he need to know about his mother? She's crazy, allergic to cats and she abandons her children when she feels like it. Even if Phil finds her, she's not someone Sid wants to know. But his brother—what was his name? Gawain. Maybe that's different.

Caleb and Phil are sitting on the porch in the faded red Adirondack chairs, having an after-dinner beer. Caleb holds one up to Sid, who shakes his head and perches on the porch railing. Beer makes him talkative and then sleepy. He wants to listen and stay alert, not babble and crash.

Caleb speaks first. "I'm curious about something." Phil's head comes up like the neighbor's pointer, Fritz, when he hears the mail truck. "What's with all the wacky names? Siddhartha, Gawain, Devi, Devorah?"

Phil laughs. "When I first met Devorah, when we first started dating, she was still calling herself Devi." He pauses and takes a swig of beer. Buying himself time, Sid thinks.

"People with bipolar disorder," Phil continues, "they get pretty passionate about things when they're in the middle of a manic episode. With Devi it was usually something spiritual. Devi is the name of a Hindu goddess. Siddhartha is the name of the Buddha. Just after I met her, she got really involved in Judaism and became Devorah. Around the time Gawain was born, she was into Arthurian legends and after that it was Celtic mysticism."

"So she's searching," Caleb says.

"I guess," Phil replies. "But she never stays with anything very long. She even went back to the church she was raised in—an Anglican cathedral—for a while last year. Called herself Debby too. It didn't suit her."

"How does she support herself?" Caleb asks. "It can't be easy—not with those kinds of issues."

"Holding down a job is hard for her," Phil agrees. "She has a friend who owns a bookstore and another with a small art gallery—she picks up work with them when she's able. After she was diagnosed, she was able to get some disability money, but it's not much. She inherited some money when her dad died; I helped her find a little house.

And she sells some of her art at her friend's gallery. Teaches a class or two when she can."

"Her art?" Sid asks. It comes out sort of high-pitched and croaky, as if his voice is still changing.

Phil looks over at Sid. "She's a mosaic artist. Has been for years. Once she got off the boat, she started messing around with broken crockery. Now she works mostly with stuff she picks up off the beach: stones and glass and shells. She can't afford to buy tiles very often. Her work is beautiful. Magical."

Megan comes out on the porch and sits on Caleb's lap. "Fariza's in bed," she says. "It's been a long day." She rests her head on Caleb's shoulder and he raises a hand to stroke her hair. "This is a lot to take in."

"Is there anyone else?" Sid asks.

Phil looks puzzled. "Anyone else?"

"Sisters, brothers, aunts and uncles, cousins—any more relatives I should know about."

"Only your grandmother," Phil replies. "Elizabeth."

"Elizabeth," Sid repeats. "Where is she?"

"In Victoria," Phil says, "searching for Wain."

I Don't Care

"Are you Gawain's dad?" Sid asks Phil at breakfast the next day.

Phil looks up, startled, from his waffles. Sid notices for the first time that Phil eyes are the same saturated blue as one of Sid's favorite Faber-Castell pens—B120.

"No, I'm not Wain's dad, although I feel like it sometimes. After we broke up, Devi and I stayed friends. My workshop is in her garage. I turned part of the garage into a tiny apartment, so I live there too."

"So where is his dad?"

"I don't know," Phil replies. "When Devi's manic, she's a bit...indiscriminate...about her men. He stuck around for a while though. Until Wain was about a year old."

"Indiscriminate," Sid repeats. "You mean she's a slut. A crazy slut."

"Sid." Megan's voice has more than a note of warning in it.

"It's okay," Phil says. "I get it."

"No, you don't," Sid says. "You come up here and tell me my birth mom's unstable and she likes to sleep around. You tell me I've got a brother and a grandmother. How can you possibly get it?"

Phil puts down his fork and levels a look at Sid that shuts him up.

"I was named after Phileas Fogg, the hero of *Around the World in Eighty Days*. My mother read it in grade-eight English, the year she got pregnant with me and her parents kicked her out. She never told anyone who my father was. I left home at sixteen, after one of my mother's boyfriends hit me one time too many. I never went back. I call my mother three times a year—on Christmas, on her birthday and on Mother's Day. She's sober now and living in the same crappy apartment I grew up in. So I get how angry and confused you are. What I want to know is this: what are you going to do about it?"

"Do about it?" Sid can hear the challenge in Phil's voice. The waffle he has just eaten rises in this throat. He swallows hard, determined not to let on how shaken he is by Phil's question. Even so, his voice is a bit unsteady when he says, "I don't know."

"Give him a bit of time, Phil," Caleb says. "This is a bit of a shock—to all of us. Devi never contacted Sid after she left. Never. As far as we're concerned, he's our son. Always will be." Sid hears the challenge in Caleb's voice.

Phil must have heard it too, because he nods and says, "Sorry, man. I'm just so worried about them. Devi will turn up sooner or later—this isn't the first time she's taken off—but Wain? He's only thirteen."

"And Sid's only sixteen," Caleb says firmly. "We'll talk about it—as a family. You're welcome to stay and answer Sid's questions, if he has any, but don't pressure him."

Caleb stands up, towering over Phil. "I'd be happy to take you out on the *Caprice*, show you a bit more of the island."

Phil takes the hint and stands as well. The top of his head only comes to Caleb's shoulder. He may be short, Sid thinks, but he's still powerful. His strength is more compact than Caleb's, possibly more explosive. Something to be aware of, even avoid.

"I'm going to the orchard," Sid announces. "If Chloe calls, can you tell her I'll come by later?"

Megan nods, and Fariza, who has been eating her waffles square by tiny square, jumps down from her chair and follows Sid to the door, Fred in tow. Today she is wearing navy-blue cut-off sweatpants and a long yellow T-shirt with a big number twelve on the back.

Going to the orchard is family code for *I need to be alone.* In Sid's case, though, he really is going to the orchard. The last thing he wants is Fariza's company. He glowers at Megan, who smiles and says, "Up to you, Sid." She knows he won't refuse, even if he wants to. He's never forgotten how lonely he felt when the older kids in the house ignored him, and the look on Fariza's face is so full of hope.

"Can you stay out of my way?" Sid asks Fariza. He already knows she can be quiet.

Fariza nods vigorously, hair beads dancing.

Sid asks, "Do you like baseball?"

Fariza's eyes widen and she nods again.

Sid runs up to his room and comes down with two baseball bats—one full size, one much smaller. "You can use this one," he says, handing Fariza the smaller bat, "but Fred has to stay home."

Fariza installs Fred on the couch with a book, slips on her Crocs and follows Sid out the door.

The orchard is a five-minute walk from the house. It isn't on Megan and Caleb's property—it belongs to a couple who live in Palm Springs. Every year Sid and Chloe help Megan and Irena pick the apples and make pie, applesauce, jelly, apple butter, fruit leather, cider. Last fall, during the apple harvest, Chloe threatened to shoot her grandmother with a tranquilizer dart and burn her collection of ancient cookbooks.

Sid comes to the orchard to think and to smack a few windfalls. He loves seeing rotten apples explode in mid-air like fermented fruit bombs. He's never wanted to play on a team, although he secretly believes he'd be the star batter if he ever tried out. His swing is powerful and his aim steady.

Today he marks out a small diamond for Fariza with some old feed sacks he finds in the run-down shed next to the orchard. He positions her at home plate, shows her how to hold the bat, and lobs a small apple at her. She swings hard, misses and falls down.

"Steee-rike one," Sid yells as Fariza dusts herself off and takes her stance again. She misses the next apple and the next, but stops falling down after the fifth strike.

"Wanna take a break?" Sid asks after her tenth strike.

Fariza answers by tapping home plate with her bat and narrowing her eyes at Sid. She raises the bat over her shoulder and Sid lobs another apple; this time she connects, although the apple remains intact. She stands stock still for a moment, bat in hand, eyes wide, and then she runs toward first base, arms pumping, hair beads clacking. Sid picks up the apple and starts to chase her— in slow motion—as she rounds second, touches third and then makes it home. She is doing a little jig on the sack, but when he swoops her up in his arms for a victory dance, she stiffens. It's like waltzing with a log.

He puts her down, and she backs away from him.

"Sorry," he says, feeling unreasonably hurt, even though Megan has explained that it's nothing personal— Fariza still freezes up when somebody male touches her. Sid doesn't know why, and he doesn't much like being lumped in with whoever hurt her.

He gathers a bunch of windfalls and picks up his own bat. "Stand back," he tells Fariza, although she is already cowering by the shed. For the next half an hour Sid tosses and pummels rotten apple after rotten apple. Most of them explode right away, but some less rotten ones really travel. Home runs, all of them, although he doesn't run the bases. After about fifteen minutes, he's not feeling hurt and angry anymore, but he's still confused. The question *Am I my brother's keeper?* flits through his mind. He shudders, and misses the next apple. Phil obviously thinks he is—or should be—his brother's, and maybe even his mother's, keeper. Why else has he come to the island? He hasn't said anything about taking Sid back to Victoria with him, but maybe that's what he wants. Sid will have to ask.

And if Phil does ask him to go, what should he say? He isn't sure. What help would he be when he got there? He wouldn't have a clue where to look. He doesn't know Gawain—who he hangs out with, where he might go. And where would he stay? With Phil? With Elizabeth, his grandmother? In Devi's vacant house? He shudders as he picks up Fariza's bat.

"Let's go," he says. She follows him, a few steps behind, all the way back to the house. When she gets inside, she runs over to Fred and burrows her face into his scrawny neck.

"You okay?" Megan calls from the War Room.

Sid leans in the doorway. "Not sure," he replies. "What do you think of Phil?"

Megan looks up from her laptop's screen. "Pretty intense. Decent guy though, I think. Cares about Devi

and Gawain." She laughs. "Gawain. Can you imagine?
Although I guess he's lucky it isn't Galahad."

"Or Merlin," Sid says.

"Or Mordred." Megan gets up, walks over to Sid
and puts her arms around him. "You and Caleb, you're
my knights in shining armor. Even if one of you is
named after the Buddha." He can smell her shampoo—
Dr. Bronner's—and feel her familiar warmth. He allows
his body to relax. Megan inhales deeply. "You smell like
cider," she says. "Was the orchard good to you?"

"Fariza hit a home run," Sid says.

"And you?" Megan asks.

Sid shrugs. "Not sure. Do you think I should go?"

"To Victoria?" Megan steps back, her hands on Sid's
forearms. "Are you ready for that?"

"I don't know," Sid says. "I don't know anything."

"Then don't make a decision. We'll talk to Phil some
more. Get a bit more information."

Sid nods. "Information. Right."

"Chloe called," Megan says. "Why don't you invite
her for lunch? She's dying to meet Phil."

"No doubt," Sid says. He can imagine how curious
Chloe is about Phil. He also knows how fearless and
persistent she can be when it comes to ferreting out
secrets. She's like a guided missile in flowery flip-flops.
Caleb says she's already a WMD—Woman of Mass
Determination—just like her mother and grandmother.
"Can we have pizza?"

Megan nods. "Pull one out of the freezer. And change your shirt. You really reek."

"Why now?" Chloe asks Phil over her first piece of pizza. As Sid could have predicted, she cuts to the chase. "I mean, why didn't you come sooner? It's been thirteen years since—what's his face—Gawain was born. Thirteen years that Sid could have known about his brother. Should have known." She glares at Phil across the table. Sid almost feels sorry for him.

"Devi didn't want me to come," Phil says. "I had to respect that. Elizabeth and I—we begged her to at least write, but she always said no. She had her reasons, I guess."

Chloe snorts. "Like what?"

Phil thinks for a moment before he speaks. "I don't like speaking for her—"

Chloe interrupts him. "But you're acting for her right now, aren't you? Is there a difference? I don't think so."

"You don't take any prisoners, do you?" Phil says. He picks up a fork and taps it rhythmically on the placemat. "But yes, I am acting for her, even though she doesn't know it. Mostly, I think, I'm acting for Wain. And for Sid."

"How so?" Chloe asks, planting her elbows on each side of her plate and resting her chin in her clasped hands. "You don't even know Sid. Devi doesn't know Sid, and he's her kid. Biologically anyway. So—back to her reasons for keeping Sid in the dark all these years. I'm listening."

Sid suppresses a laugh. Chloe's posture and language come straight from their school's guidance counselor: impatience (and an agenda) masked with concern.

"Devi knows she was a poor parent to Sid—"

"Poor?" Chloe's voice rises. "That's putting it mildly."

"You gonna interrupt me every time I open my mouth?" Phil asks.

Chloe shakes her head and mimes zipping her lips together.

Phil continues. "She also knew that she did the right thing—giving Sid up. Leaving the island. At that point, she hadn't been diagnosed. Her life was chaos. She couldn't provide a stable home for Sid—she knew that. They were living on a leaky old boat, for chrissakes! She never told anyone but me about Sid. Not her mother, not Wain. But she got drunk once, years ago, and showed me a lock of his hair and a photograph of him as a baby. When she sobered up, and I asked her about it, she swore me to secrecy."

Chloe opens her mouth to speak, and Phil holds up his hand like a Stop sign.

"By the time she got pregnant with Gawain, she'd been diagnosed and placed on a bunch of different medications, trying to find a combination that worked. Against her doctors' advice, she went off her meds. It was rough, but she hadn't had a major episode for a while and the pregnancy went okay. But she couldn't risk bringing Sid into the mix. It would have been too much.

She went back on her meds for a while after Wain's first birthday, when his father left her. But she hated the side effects. She tried to control her moods with alternative stuff: herbal remedies, meditation, yoga. Up until about a year ago, she's been pretty good, but Wain's a handful. She had to go back on her meds."

Chloe raises her hand, as if she's in school. Phil nods.

"How is Wain a handful?" she asks.

"He's started hanging out with an older crowd. Cutting school, staying out all night, getting into fights. The cops brought him home one night after he was caught stealing cheese, of all things. He said he had a sudden craving for extra-old cheddar."

Megan, who has been silent so far, says, "I can imagine his mother would be freaking out."

"She was," Phil replies, "and she blamed herself, of course. The meds have a lot of side effects. She thought maybe Wain would do better if she was more alert, more involved in his life. She worried that she hadn't been paying enough attention to him. It didn't make any sense to me—she's a good mother. Better than most. Until she went cold turkey a few weeks ago."

"Cold turkey?" Megan sounds shocked. "That's terrible."

"I know," Phil says. "It was. She had a full-blown manic episode, trashed her house and disappeared. Wain came home from school one day and she was gone. Two weeks later, he was gone too. So I decided to break the silence. I hope I've done the right thing."

"But I still don't get why you're here," Chloe says. "What does any of this have to do with Sid?"

Phil waits a long time before speaking. "Elizabeth asked me to come. Over the years, she and I have gotten pretty close. She wants to meet Sid. For some reason, she thinks he'll be able to find Wain. It's not logical, but there you have it. She's not a woman you argue with. And she is his grandmother."

"Even so," Megan says, "it's a lot to ask. Of Sid. Of us. After all this time. We don't know you—or Elizabeth. Sid's not going anywhere unless we feel it's safe." Caleb reaches out and puts his large hand over Megan's small one.

"It's gonna be okay, hon," he says. "We're just talking. Nothing's been set in stone. And Sid doesn't have to go if he doesn't want to. Right, Phil?"

Phil nods and takes a drink of water.

Chloe stands up and leans across the table toward Phil, her eyes narrowing. Sid can tell she's about to explode; he stands beside her and puts his arm around her shoulders, pulling her back from the table.

"He belongs here," Chloe says. "With his family. With me. Not in Victoria with some—some lunatic and her juvie son."

"It's okay, Chloe," he says. "Like Caleb said, we're just talking. Nobody's saying I have to do anything." He looks around the table at Phil and Megan and Caleb. "Right, guys?"

They all nod, but Chloe pulls away from Sid and rockets out of the rooms, slamming the front door. They can hear her pound down the stairs. In the silence that follows her exit, Caleb lets out a huge sigh, as if he has been underwater for a long time.

"What'd I tell you," he says to Phil. "WMD."

Watch Your Step

"Are you sure, Sid?" Megan is sitting on Sid's bed, watching him fold his clothes and stuff them in his backpack.

"No," Sid replies. "Not really. But I'm curious. I mean—a brother. And a grandmother. I gotta go, right?" What was it Irena always said to Chloe? *Curiosity killed the cat.* Sid hopes this proves not to be true.

"Are you scared?" Megan reaches out and puts her hand on Sid's arm.

"Yeah. A bit." Sid pauses in his packing. He's more than scared—he's terrified—but lately he's been thinking a lot about what Tobin said just before he left: *If you don't watch out, you're going to turn into some phobic hermit Unabomber weirdo.* Sid knows Tobin had a good point.

If he doesn't break away from his routines soon, he never will. Looking for a lost brother seems like a good way to try. It feels horrible though, as if he is gutting himself with one of Caleb's fileting knives.

"I wouldn't go if she was there, you know," he says as he rolls up yet another black T-shirt.

"If who was there?"

"Devi, Devorah, Debby. I never want to see her. You're my mother. Caleb's my father. I just want you to know I'm clear on that." He clears his throat as tears sting his eyes.

Megan is silent for a moment.

"Thank you, Sid," she finally says. "But if you want to see her, that's okay too. It's up to you. It won't change anything between us. We always wondered if Devi might turn up one day. It used to scare me, but not anymore. You've been our son for fourteen years. That's a long time. And it sounds like she's had a rough life."

Sid shrugs. He wonders if there is something wrong with him—not wanting to meet his birth mother, not caring about her. He knows that lots of adopted children long for their biological parents, but he never has. Megan took him to a play therapist when he was about four and didn't want to go to pre-school. The therapist worked with him once a week for a few months and concluded that he had a bit of what she called social anxiety but nothing to be concerned about.

He skipped kindergarten but went relatively cheer-fully to grade one. By then, he and Chloe had become friends, so everyone relaxed: Sid was okay. A bit odd, maybe, but okay. Not fucked up—at least not any more than most kids. Now he wonders if bipolar disorder is an inherited disease. Although he's rarely, if ever, felt manic, the thought is still unsettling.

"I feel bad about Fariza," Sid says to Megan. "I feel like I'm abandoning her." He's never worried about another kid before, but Fariza is different. He wonders if this is what he'll feel like with Wain: protective, concerned, guilty.

"I know," Megan replies. "But she's not your respon-sibility, you know. It's great that she's so comfortable with you, but she'll manage, I promise."

"You think?"

Megan nods. "It's going to be a long time before she gets over what happened to her, if she ever does, but I think she knows she's safe here. And we'll talk about you every day. I'll remind her that you're coming back."

"Okay." Sid's backpack is stuffed to overflowing. He puts it on the floor and sits beside Megan on the bed. "I gave Fariza a sketchbook of her own. We work on it every day."

"I know," Megan says.

"I divided a whole bunch of pages for her. Enough for a couple of weeks. I drew myself coming home on the last page, so she won't forget. Could you help her write a story a day in the bottom box of every page? When I come back, I'll illustrate it for her."

"Sure, sweetie," Megan says. "No problem. And maybe you could call—check in every now and again. Even if she doesn't talk, I'm sure she'd like to hear your voice." She laughs. "Oh, who am I kidding? I'd like to hear your voice."

"How about I call every other day around suppertime?"

"Sounds like a plan," Megan says. "You ready?"

"Ready as I'll ever be." Sid hoists his backpack over one shoulder and pulls Megan into an awkward hug with his other arm.

"Onward and upward," Megan mumbles into his armpit.

Sid throws his backpack into the back of Miss Havisham and gets into the front seat as Phil says his goodbyes to Megan and Caleb and Fariza. Chloe hasn't spoken to Sid since he told her he was going, so she isn't here to say goodbye. He has left email and phone messages telling her he'll be back soon, but she remains as silent as Fariza, who is standing with one arm wrapped around Megan's waist and the other arm clutching Fred.

"Bye, Fariza," Sid calls. "See you soon. Don't forget to draw in your book."

He waves jauntily at her, trying to look cheerful rather than upset. She gives him a small smile and then buries her face in Megan's side. He feels like the worst person in the world. Selfish. Inconsiderate. Foolish. But also excited. And more than a little anxious.

"Ready?" Phil slides into the driver's seat and puts on his sunglasses.

Sid nods, and Phil backs out of the driveway. Sid doesn't look back. He is silent on the ride to the ferry. He stays in the car when they get on board, while Phil goes up to the passenger lounge. Sid shuts his eyes and slumps down in the seat. He doesn't want to see the familiar scenery slip by: the red wharf, the white fish boats, the green islet in the cove, the blue water, the ferry's frothy wake. He doesn't want to hear the squeak of the ferry against the pilings, the clang of the ramp coming up, the casual chatter between passengers as they make their way upstairs. There's a great audio system in the car. Maybe he should dig out his iPod and plug it in. Phil's iPod is sitting in the well between the seats. Between them, they probably have more than enough music for the five-hour trip. Sid prays that Phil isn't a fan of either Dixieland or disco. Anything else he can stand, although he wonders how Phil feels about Foo Fighters or Mother Mother.

As they near the other side, Phil returns to the car and they sit in silence, waiting for the ramp to come down and connect them to the next part of their journey.

"You go to Victoria very often?" Phil asks.

"Nope," Sid says. "Usually Vancouver. Megan likes Ikea."

Phil laughs. "Who doesn't?"

"Me," Sid says. "Too crowded. Too noisy."

"Gotcha." Phil is silent for a few minutes, but as they reach the turnoff to the highway, he says, "You always such a hard-ass?"

Sid laughs. "You think I'm a hard-ass?" No one has ever called him anything like that.

"Well, aren't you? The silent treatment's pretty harsh."

"It's not meant to be," Sid says, although this is a bit of a lie. He really doesn't want to talk to Phil. Phil is the messenger, and Sid still isn't sure whether to shoot him or welcome him. "It's not personal. I'm just not much of a talker." No way he's going to tell Phil that he feels like he's going to puke.

"I got that." Phil shoots him a sideways glance. "But we've got a long ride ahead of us—you might want to throw me a bone."

"How would I do that?" Sid asks, genuinely curious.

"Tell me about growing up on the island, about your art, about your ambitions. Tell me what music you listen to, what books you love."

"We could just listen to the music I like," Sid says, gesturing at the audio system. "For a while anyway."

Phil considers this for a minute and then says,
"Fine. Your music until we hit Nanaimo, mine between
Nanaimo and Duncan and then conversation from
Duncan to Victoria. That'll give you a lot of time to
think of things to talk about. Deal?"

"Deal," Sid says as he plugs in his iPod.

"Jingle Pot Road," Phil says.

Sid, who has been thinking about Chloe and wishing
she had come to say goodbye, turns down the music.
"What did you say?"

"Jingle Pot Road. We just passed it. We're in Nanaimo,
land of strip malls, abandoned coal mines and weird place
names. Can you imagine living on Buttertubs Marsh or
Dingle Bingle Hill? Makes you wonder what those coal
miners were smoking."

Sid laughs. Phil is intense, but even Sid has to admit
he's a good travel companion. They had stopped at a
wide beach near Parksville to eat the lunch Megan
packed for them, sitting side by side on a log and
watching whole families almost vanish on the shim-
mering tidal flats. Plastic shovels and tiny sneakers lay
in the sand next to pails full of sand dollars. Sid worried
that the sea would swallow them. He remembers losing
his favorite sand toy—a yellow plastic bulldozer—on
this beach. He and Megan and Caleb had walked what

seemed to him miles and miles to the water's edge. When they got back, the bulldozer was gone. He had been inconsolable, and even now he feels a twinge of the distress he felt at four. It was, he thinks, the first time he had lost something that really mattered to him. Unless he counts his mother, which he doesn't.

After they leave Nanaimo, Sid falls asleep to some peculiar, but oddly soothing, music that sounds vaguely Celtic, but also vaguely Asian. When he wakes up, the car is parked at a Dairy Queen in Duncan. Phil is nowhere to be seen.

Sid orders a Blizzard with Reese's Pieces and sits at a picnic table outside to eat it. Phil comes out of the bathroom, gets a hot fudge sundae and sits down across from Sid.

"There is a god," Phil states, spooning up a mouthful of his sundae.

"If you say so," Sid says, although he's inclined, at this moment, to agree.

"You can start anytime," Phil says.

"Start what?"

"The Life and Times of Siddhartha Eikenboom. We're in Duncan, in case you hadn't noticed."

"I noticed."

"So—we had a deal."

Sid scrapes the bottom of his Blizzard cup with the long red plastic spoon. He considers ordering another but knows it will make him sick.

sarah n. harvey

"Can I take a leak first?" he asks.

Phil nods. "I'll be waiting."

It's surprisingly easy to talk to Phil. Even though he keeps his attention on the road, Sid knows he's listening from the way he laughs or asks for clarification or says, "You're kidding!" every now and again. Sid finds himself tempted to make stuff up, but Phil seems interested in the boring details of Sid's life. It turns out they can both quote whole scenes from *Back to the Future*; Phil almost drives off the road when Sid does his impersonation of Marty McFly: *Time circuits on. Flux capacitor...fluxing. Engine running. All right.*

"You got some talent, man," Phil gasps.

"Thanks, dude," Sid replies as the car straightens out. "But I don't wanna die for it."

As they approach the outskirts of Victoria, Sid stops talking and Phil doesn't push him to chat. When they finally turn into an unpaved driveway on a narrow tree-lined street, Sid is unsure he can get out of the car. His legs feel like overcooked pasta. Phil turns off the engine and they sit, listening to the engine tick as it cools.

"That's Devi's place," Phil says, pointing at a ramshackle cottage set way off the road, surrounded by about a zillion oak trees. Sid is glad he'll be gone before the leaves start to fall. The raking must be brutal. "I'm in the garage

64

at the back," Phil continues. "I thought you could stay out there, and I'll bunk at Devi's."

A huge marmalade cat ambles up to the car, and Phil gets out and drapes it across his shoulders like a feather boa. An ancient gray cat with milky eyes brushes against his ankles, and Phil scoops it up too and cradles it in his arms. A tabby with a stump for a tail approaches across the lawn. Sid gets out of the car and crouches down to stroke it.

"Which is which?" he asks.

"That's Smike," Phil says. He nuzzles the cat in his arms. "This old guy is Dodger, and the one that thinks he's a scarf is Fagin. Fagin runs the show, but keep an eye on the Dodger—he's still got some tricks, don't you, Dodge?" As if in answer, Dodger takes a swipe at Fagin's tail. "Grab your bag from the back and let's get you settled."

Phil goes ahead of Sid and opens the garage door. When Sid gets inside, he stops, looks around and inhales deeply. The garage is full of tools and wood and sawdust and half-completed pieces of furniture. And it smells amazing—like coffee and glue and solvent and wood chips, with a hint of beer and a whiff of sweat. Sid thinks if you could make a men's cologne that smelled like Phil's garage, you'd make a fortune. Call it Varnish or Grain and sell it at Home Depot in vials shaped like nail guns or power drills.

The living quarters are screened off from the work-shop by an ornate Japanese screen. Phil shows Sid the bed in the loft, the minute kitchen, the microscopic bath-room. Skylights illuminate each room. Phil feeds the cats and then opens a bag of chips, dumps a jar of salsa into a blue bowl and takes a can of Coke out of the fridge.

"I'm going to check things out over at Devi's. And I need to give Elizabeth a call. You okay on your own for a bit?"

Sid takes a swig of Coke. "Sure. I'm okay. Do what you have to do."

After Phil leaves, Sid sits down at the beat-up oak table and rests his head in his folded arms. He doesn't think he has ever been so tired, even though he's been sitting almost all day. He remembers Megan telling him once that anxiety can be as tiring as running a triathalon.

"If that's true, I'm Simon fucking Whitfield," he mutters as he rests. "Where's my gold medal?"

Make My Day

When Sid wakes up the next day, a seagull is crapping on the skylight above his head. He hopes it isn't an omen. He's not particularly superstitious, but even simple things, like a sudden downpour or a lost sock, seem portentous—even ominous—these days. He vaguely remembers climbing the ladder to the loft the night before, and he has slept surprisingly well. He can hear Phil in the kitchen talking to the cats. He can smell bacon.

"Hope you're not a vegetarian," Phil says as Sid comes down the ladder. "Or, god forbid, a vegan." He shudders.

"Nope. Love bacon. Eggs too. Breakfast's my favorite meal. Need any help?"

"Nah. It's under control. And this kitchen is built for one. You've got time for a shower. I put out clean towels."

Sid nods and goes into the tiny bathroom. It reminds him of the bathroom on the *Caprice*—designed to waste no space. Except Phil's bathroom has walls that look like wooden patchwork quilts, and the inside of the shower stall is covered in a mosaic of deadly sea creatures—jellyfish, octopi, sharks, stingrays, barracuda, stonefish, spiny sea urchins. Devi's work, Sid assumes. He has to admit, it is beautiful, if a bit bizarre. When he comes out, his ringlets dripping onto his clean T-shirt, Phil serves up breakfast, which they eat in silence.

When they are finished, Sid cleans up. It's the least he can do, he thinks, and it kills a bit more time. He's not sure he's ready for whatever comes next. He wants to go up to the loft, crawl back into bed and watch the sky for signs. An eagle, a balloon, a jet trail. His stomach is already churning. He wonders if coming here was a mistake.

"I called Elizabeth last night," Phil says. "No sign of Wain. Or Devi. You ready to meet your grandmother?"

"I guess," Sid says. "Can I see a picture of them first?" He doesn't know why he hasn't thought to ask before, but he hopes that seeing what they look like will ease the sense of dread that is creeping up his limbs, weakening his resolve.

"Sure, "Phil says. "Good idea." He rummages in a kitchen drawer and pulls out a drugstore photo envelope. "I took these at Wain's birthday last March. We all pitched in and got him that Guitar Hero thing."

He hands the envelope to Sid, who pulls out the photos. On top is a picture of a small woman with short gray curls and a plump, unlined face. She has her arm around a tall thin elderly woman with white hair in an elegant French twist. Beside them is a tall heavyset boy with close-cropped curls, a huge grin and a red guitar. He is a bit blurry, but not so blurry that Sid can't see that he is black. Inky black. Whoa. All along, he's been picturing Gawain as a miniature version of himself: red-haired, pale, wiry, quiet. Clearly, this boy isn't any of those things. He looks like a football player—a linebacker maybe. Sid knows nothing about football—soccer is his game. Even if they do find Wain, what will Sid have to say to him?

He hands the photos back to Phil. "Let's go," he says. "I'll look at the rest later."

Phil slides the photos back in the drawer and grabs his keys.

"You'll like Elizabeth," he says.

Phil is right. Sid does like Elizabeth. From the moment she greets him at the door of her condo, he feels at ease. She answers the door in soft coffee-colored cords and a beige cashmere sweater. On her feet are suede moccasins with rabbit trim and fancy beadwork on the toes, and around her neck hangs a silver Celtic knot on a leather thong. Her hair is gathered into a low ponytail secured by a red silk scarf. When he hears her intake of breath when she sees him, he realizes that he is holding his breath.

"Welcome," she says, stepping aside to let them enter. Sid stands in the foyer, wondering if he should take off his shoes. He's not used to houses as pristine and white as this one.

"Don't worry about your shoes," Elizabeth says, as if he has spoken aloud. "Come in, come in."

Sid follows her into the living room. Phil disappears into the kitchen, muttering something about fixing a dripping faucet. The view of the harbor is unobstructed, and Sid goes to the window and watches a floatplane land near some kayakers. Elizabeth stands beside him and says, "There's always something going on. I never get tired of it. "

Sid nods. "I do that at home—watch the harbor."

"Better than TV," Elizabeth says with a laugh. "And no commercials. Although commercials have been very good to me."

"Good to you?" Sid is puzzled. He hardly ever watches TV and when he does he finds most of the commercials annoying.

"After my husband—your grandfather, Stan—died, I was unhappy and bored. I tried lots of old-lady things— bridge, mall-walking, bird-watching. Nothing took my fancy. Then I saw that 'Where's the beef?' commercial and I got to thinking—maybe there's a market out there for little-old-lady actors. So I found an agent and started going after the juicy parts: daft old things with ill-fitting dentures, ancient biddies in need of home care, spunky grannies who dance and rap, nasty old bats carrying wicked canes. I'll do anything on camera—rollerblade, paraglide, mountain bike, scuba dive—anything but die. I draw the line at that."

Sid stares at her, and then the penny drops. "You're the Gray Matter Granny!" he says. "I love those commercials. That one where you were hang gliding was awesome."

Elizabeth curtsies. "Thank you, my dear. Who knew geriatric vitamins could be so much fun? Or so lucrative. Next year we're going on location in Hawaii—geezers in paradise, I call it. I'll be surfing and biking down a volcano and hula dancing." She makes a fluttering motion with her hands and swivels her hips.

Sid smiles and says, "Aloha." He turns away from the window and looks around the condo. Everything in it looks brand-new. He had expected antiques and heirlooms, potpourri and gilt-framed pictures of sour-looking ancestors. Faded Oriental carpets, the smell of talcum powder. He couldn't have been more wrong.

As if anticipating a question she has been asked many times before, Elizabeth says, "After Stan died, I sold the big house and put everything except my clothes in storage. I furnished this entire place—dishes, rugs, candleholders, soap dishes, towels—from the IKEA catalog. Once in a while I dream about Stan doing something around the old house—putting up a picture, pouring a glass of wine, unloading the dishwasher. When I wake up, I go to the storage locker and find an object from the dream and it becomes part of my waking life again. The last thing I brought back was his old wooden Slazenger tennis racquet. I dreamed he was using the side of the house as a backboard again. It used to drive me crazy. I hope I never dream that he's dusting the figurine collection I inherited from my Great-Aunt Harriet. She had very bad taste in trinkets. I think I'm fairly safe though; Stan never dusted anything in his life." She laughs, but there is a quaver in her voice.

"Is that him?" Sid asks, pointing at a framed photograph on a side table.

Elizabeth pulls a cloth hankie from her sweater cuff, wipes her eyes and says, "Yes. On our twentieth anniversary." She hands Sid the photograph and he notices that her hand is vibrating slightly, like a tuning fork. He wonders if she's as nervous as he is. Or maybe she has—what's it called?—Parkinson's. One of Irena's friends has it and her head moves almost all the time, like a bobble-head doll on a dashboard. He sneaks a look at Elizabeth's head, which sits peacefully at the top of her long neck. No bobble. The relief he feels is strange and welcome. He hardly knows her, but he wants her to be well and happy.

He looks down at the photo she has given him. A tall man in gray flannel pants, a navy blazer and a crisp, pale-blue shirt gazes out at him, smiling slightly, a drink in one hand, a cigarette in the other. His tie has been loosened. He is standing in a garden next to a wrought-iron bench. Behind him are tall purple and pink flowers. Hollyhocks, Sid thinks. Megan's favorite.

"You have the same eyes," Elizabeth says. Sid looks more closely and sees that she is right. His grandfather's eyes, like his, are pale gray—the gray of a morning fog—with a black ring around the iris. Unlike Sid, Stan has thick black hair and bushy black eyebrows.

"He was nicknamed Groucho when he was a little boy," Elizabeth says. "At least you've escaped that fate. The red hair is from my side of the family—the Gallaghers were all wild Irish redheads."

"I remember her hair," Sid says. "Devi's hair."

"Her hair was glorious," Elizabeth says. "Like yours. But it's gray now. And short."

"Yeah. I saw a picture. Of her and Wain and you."

When he doesn't continue, Elizabeth says, "It's all a bit of a shock, isn't it?"

"Yup," Sid says, thinking of Wain's blue-black skin, his white grin. "Did you really not know about me?" It's hard for him to imagine keeping such an enormous secret for so long, although if he is honest, he knows he's probably capable of it. He wonders how Devi felt after she left him with Megan. Ashamed? Worthless? Sad? Even so—not telling your own mother that you have a child—that's huge. And kind of cruel.

"The first I heard of you was a week ago, when Wain disappeared and Phil decided to tell me Devi's secret. He's been a good friend to her—and to me—but I wish he hadn't waited so long to tell me." Elizabeth reaches over and touches Sid lightly on the arm. "But you're here now—that's what's important, yes?"

"I guess," he says. "I'm not really sure why I'm here though. I mean, how am I going to find Wain when you and Phil can't?"

"I don't know, dear," Elizabeth says. "Mostly I just wanted to meet you. I'm sorry if that seems selfish. And we can certainly use your help trying to find Wain. The police are aware that he's run away, but he's run away so many times, I don't think they're looking all that hard. He's never been gone this long though. And with Devi gone...well, I'm not as young as I used to be and I don't have the energy to go out after dark and search for him. Wain and I aren't as close as we once were. I don't know his friends anymore. Or where he might go."

"But I don't know him at all," Sid says. "And I don't know the city either."

Elizabeth sits on the couch and pats the cushion beside her.

"Sit down, and I'll tell you about him. Maybe that will help."

Sid turns back to the window. TMI, he thinks. That's what Chloe would say. Too Much Information. He needs some time to take it all in. A huge gray ferry with a red stripe near the waterline is angling into the harbor—*Coho*, it says on the bow. It looks impossibly large for the space, a Godzilla of a ship about to crush the tiny wharf.

Miraculously, it doesn't. "I'd rather go for walk," he says. "If that's okay with you."

Armed with a school photo of Wain and a map of downtown Victoria, Sid sets out alone, promising to be back by lunchtime. Phil says he has things to do and that he will pick Sid up after lunch. Sid worries that Elizabeth is already disappointed in him, but he needs to be alone. She can tell him about Wain over lunch.

When he comes out of the condo building, he turns left and follows a waterfront walkway in front of a hotel and onto a pale-blue bridge that looks like it's constructed of rusty Meccano. The pedestrian path is made of wooden planks that vibrate slightly as the cars go by on the other side of a metal railing. There is a red wharf to the right, and Sid smiles at the sight of it. Just like home. He can see people on a grassy verge above the wharf. Maybe he should talk to them about Wain. But as he approaches them, he realizes that they are homeless men, much older than Wain, dirty, some obviously drunk or high. Sid turns away and heads up the street. He passes small stores selling expensive clothing and explores a brick courtyard where a juggler is entertaining a crowd of kids. He knows he should be showing people the picture of Wain, but he's not ready yet. Besides, most of the people in the courtyard look like tourists: souvenir T-shirts, cameras, tourist maps.

He needs to find some local teenagers, but right now he is content to wander. Just before it's time to head back to Elizabeth's, he goes into an art supply store and treats himself to a new set of colored pens and a small sketchbook. Megan had slipped him $200 before he left. For necessities or emergencies, she said. He left his sketchbook locked up at home, but now he wants to draw the blue bridge, the juggler, the monstrous ferry, the kayakers. He figures this counts as a necessity, if not an emergency. Around the corner from the art supply store is a bakery. He remembers that Megan always brings a small gift when she's invited to someone's house for a meal. He buys half a dozen cookies from a girl about his own age, with spiky platinum hair and a ring through one eyebrow. As she is counting out his change, he pulls out the picture of Wain.

"Have you seen this kid?" he asks.

She peers at the picture for a long moment and then says, "Who is he?"

"My brother. He's missing."

"You're kidding."

Sid can't tell if she's responding to the fact that Wain is missing or that he's Sid's brother.

"Half brother, yeah. He's been missing for a week."

The girl shakes her head. "Sorry, no. Haven't seen him."

Sid pockets the picture and picks up his bag of cookies. He feels deflated, although he knows it's ridiculous to think that finding Wain would be as easy as showing his picture to one person.

"I'll let you know if I see him," the girl says.

"That'd be great," Sid says. He turns to walk out of the bakery, and she grabs his sleeve, laughing.

"Name? Phone number?" she says.

Sid blushes as she holds out a scrap of paper and a pencil. "My name's Sid. I'm staying with my grandmother, Elizabeth Eikenboom. She lives over by that hotel on the harbor. I don't know her phone number." He feels like a dolt. He should have thought to get Elizabeth's phone number before he left.

"No cell?"

"Me? No. They don't work where I live."

"Where do you live? Outer Mongolia?"

Sid laughs. "No. On an island up north."

The girl nods. "That explains it then."

"Explains what?"

"Your air of—I dunno—mystery. Maybe a whiff of innocence."

Sid blushes again as the girl sticks out her hand to shake his.

"I'm Amie. With an *ie*. Like French for friend," she says, rolling her eyes. "My little sister's name, Harmonie, also with an *ie*. I won't tell you what my mother's name is. It's too embarrassing. I'm here seven to twelve, Wednesday to Sunday. If you bring me a copy of that picture, I'll ask around. And we could look for him together too."

"You'd do that?" Sid says. "Why?"

Amie laughs. "Because you look lost. Because I'm a sucker for redheads. Because your brother is so young. Because I'm bored. Pick one. Anyway, it's kinda tough if you don't know the scene."

"The scene?"

"You know. Where kids hang out. Where not to go. That kind of thing."

A customer clears his throat behind Sid, who steps aside to let him order.

When in Doubt

"I made Wain's favorite lunch," Elizabeth tells him when he arrives back at the condo. "Cheese dreams and apple boats."

"Sounds good," Sid says, although he has no idea what a cheese dream is. "I brought cookies." He holds the bag out to Elizabeth.

"How thoughtful," she says. "Now go wash up and I'll pop the cheese dreams under the broiler."

It turns out that cheese dreams are what Megan calls cheese toasties: English muffins, cheddar cheese and bacon broiled until the cheese melts and the bacon crisps. Bacon twice in one day, Sid thinks. That would never happen at home.

"I used to ask Megan to make these all the time," Sid says. "She didn't use English muffins—no white flour in our house—and we had them with applesauce. But apple boats are good too," he hastens to add. "If the apples aren't mushy."

"Agreed," Elizabeth says. "There's nothing worse than a mushy apple."

They eat in silence for a few minutes. Elizabeth hasn't yet asked about his morning. She seems very calm for someone whose daughter and grandson are missing. Maybe she's a naturally calm person or maybe she's had to learn to be calm, with a crazy daughter and an out-of-control grandson. Sid isn't used to taking the lead in conversations, but he wants her to know that he made a bit of progress, if you can call it that.

"I met a girl today who says she'll help me look for Wain," Sid says. "Her name's Amie. She works at the bakery where I got the cookies."

Elizabeth nods.

"So could I have some more copies of Wain's picture? And I need a contact number for people too."

"You should have a phone while you're here," Elizabeth says. "One of those throwaway phones criminals always use on TV." She smiles. "Although you don't look like much of a criminal to me."

"A burner phone, you mean?" Sid says, thinking of his shrinking two hundred dollars.

"Is that what they're called? I'll ask Phil where to get one. And don't worry. I'll pay for it."

Sid starts to stutter that he can pay, but he doesn't sound very convincing, even to himself.

"I'm a rich old lady, Sid," Elizabeth says. "And you're my grandson. I have some indulging to catch up on."

"Okay. But I don't need, like, an iPhone or anything. There's no service on the island. And I'm not going to be here very long."

"I understand," Elizabeth says, and Sid believes her.

Phil buys Sid a phone at a 7-Eleven, and when they get back to the garage, Sid goes up to the loft and calls Chloe. He knows it's long distance, but he doesn't care. He needs to talk to her. Of course, she doesn't answer her cell; even if she is in an area that gets service, his number will show up as *Unknown*. He leaves her a message. "It's me. I have a cell. Yeah, I know. I said I'd never get one, but I need one down here. Call me. Please. I miss you. I know you're mad at me for leaving, and I'm sorry." He leaves his number, disconnects and then phones home. Megan doesn't pick up either. He leaves his number again, feeling lonelier than he has since he left the island. He climbs down the ladder and watches Phil sand a chest of drawers.

"No luck?" Phil looks up and stops sanding.

Sid shakes his head. "Is there a bike I could use?" he asks. "I thought I'd go for a ride. Check out the 'hood."

"My bike has two flat tires—I don't use it much—but you can take Devi's sit-up-and-beg or Wain's BMX."

"Sit-up-and-beg?" Sid has never heard of such a thing. It sounds like a dog, not a bike.

"You know, a ladies' bike with a low bar, high handlebars and a chain guard. Devi's bike is hot pink and it has a wicker carrier basket. And a bell." Phil grins.

Sid shudders. He'd rather crawl on his hands and knees than ride a bike like that. "What about Wain's bike? He's big for thirteen. Should be okay." Sid wishes he'd thought to bring his dirty gray mountain bike with him. BMX bikes always feel strange to him—as if he's stolen a bike from a six-year-old.

"It's on the back porch," Phil says. "He loved that bike. For a while he talked about getting into competitive riding—he's really good—but lately it's just been sitting on the porch, gathering dust."

"Cool." Sid heads out the door. "When should I be back?"

"Couple of hours," Phil says. "I thought we'd order in some pizza, strategize."

"Strategize?"

"About Wain."

"Right," Sid says as he shuts the door behind him.

Wain's bike is bright green and expensive. The words *The Green Knight* are written in an old-fashioned script on the bottom bar. Sid laughs. *Sir Gawain and the Green Knight*. Awesome. He still has an illustrated version of the old tale from when he was about ten. He remembers how the Green Knight put his severed head back on his shoulders, how Gawain confronted an ogre, a dragon, a pack of wolves. How it all turned out well in the end. He swings the bike off the porch, checks its tires and rides down the bumpy driveway to the street, feeling like a giant on a midget's bike.

He turns left and then right, heading for the ocean. At least he thinks he is. He figures he can't go too far wrong—they are on an island, after all. A bigger island than he lives on but still an island. A few blocks later he can smell the sea, and he follows a road that winds along the shoreline. He passes a marina with a life-size model of a killer whale out front. Next to the marina is a small park. A mile or so farther is another park, this one with a children's playground and a long promenade. He stops to watch some kids making a sandcastle, and then continues up a hill to another park with a boat launch. He rides the Green Knight over the rocks to the water and watches some sailboats race across the choppy waves toward an orange buoy. In the distance to his left is an enormous snow-capped mountain. It looks, improbably, like a postcard of Mount Fuji propped up on the horizon. He'll have to ask Phil its name. He thinks it might be in the United States, but he's not sure. All he knows is that everything here feels both familiar and strange at the same time. The same coast, but different. If he rode his bike for half an hour at home, he would be in the wilderness, or close to it. Here, after a half-hour bike ride, he is still surrounded by the evidence of civilization: waterfront mansions, suvs, tour buses, well-dressed women walking designer dogs on fancy leashes. Overflowing trash cans. Hip-hop blasting from a car stereo. And yet, the rocks, the sky, the water, the wind, the sun—all the same. He imagines the water rushing up the narrow strait from here to the island. If he threw a message in a bottle into the fast-moving whirlpools here, maybe Chloe would pick it up in the cove. Maybe she would reply. He needs to talk to her: about Elizabeth, about his dead grandfather, about the Green Knight.

He sits for a while, watching the boats navigate the orange buoy, listening to the gulls fight over some garbage, and then hops on the bike and heads back to Phil's.

"It's not really much of a strategy," Sid says to Amie the next day. "More like a plan. In the daytime, I'm going to spend some time downtown, show Wain's picture around. At night, Phil will drive around, talk to people."

Amie's shift at the bakery is over and she wants to get some sushi before they start searching for Wain.

"Did you bring more pictures?" she asks. "We need to hand them out."

Sid nods. "Elizabeth printed out a bunch for me. She's got everything—iMac, photo printer, fax machine, digital camera. She says she needs it for her career."

"Her career? Isn't she, like, eighty?"

"More like seventy, I think. She's an actor. You've probably seen her—she does a lot of commercials."

"Like what?"

"Well, she's the Gray Matter Granny." Sid feels ridiculously proud when he says this, as if Elizabeth had won the Nobel Prize for peace.

"No kidding! I love that shit. It's all over YouTube. Does she know that?"

"I doubt it," Sid says. "I don't think she's a big YouTube watcher."

He doesn't add that neither is he. "Anyway, I put my cell number on the backs of all the pictures."

"Good plan," Amie says. She stops in front of a sushi restaurant. "My friend Dan works here. Come and meet him. We can ask him about Wain."

Sid expects Dan to be Asian, but he looks like he belongs on a California beach: long messy blond hair, serious tan, blue eyes, straight white teeth. A young Keanu Reeves with a bad dye-job.

"Here's your tuna roll, Ames," he says, handing Amie a brown paper bag. "Extra soy sauce. This the guy you were telling me about?"

Amie nods. "This is Sid. Sid, this is Dan."

Dan raises a fist in greeting and taps Sid on the shoulder. "I hear you lost your baby bro."

"You could say that," Sid replies. "Although I've never actually met him, so it's kinda weird to say I've lost him.

But yeah, he's missing. Has been for about a week. He's only thirteen."

"Harsh," Dan says. "That's young. You got a visual?"

"A what?"

"An image. A picture."

Sid pulls one of the photographs of Wain out of his backpack and hands it to Dan, who does a double take.

"Dude, he's black," Dan says, as if it might have escaped Sid's notice.

"Duh," Amie says. "And your mother's Korean. What's your point?"

"Nothin'," Dan says. "I was surprised, is all. I mean, look at him." He points at Sid. "Doesn't get much whiter than that." He jabs a thick finger at the picture of Wain. "Or much blacker than that. I'm just sayin'."

"Point taken," Sid says, edging toward the door.

Amie pays Dan and follows Sid out the door. "Sorry about that," she says. "He's a good guy. Just not all that… subtle."

"I picked up on that," Sid says. "Being a subtle guy myself."

Amie laughs and pulls a black plastic tray of sushi out of the bag. "Can we sit for a minute while I eat?"

"Sure," Sid says. "Where?"

"Here is good." Amie says, pointing at a bench outside a Starbucks. "I come here all the time. We should leave a picture with them."

Sid goes inside while she eats. The kid at the counter takes the picture without looking at it.

He gets a similar response at most of the places they go that afternoon. No one seems very interested, or concerned. "He's only thirteen," Sid says over and over. "Looks older," one woman says in an accusatory tone, as if Sid is lying.

"What's wrong with people?" he asks Amie when they stop to get a drink from a street vendor.

She shrugs. "Burnt out maybe. Lots of kids come here when they run away. Get into drugs, hooking, panhandling. Stores get broken into, pissed on, vandalized. The retailers get a bit paranoid. He's just another runaway to them. Potential trouble."

Sid wonders how bad your home life would have to be to want to sleep on the cold concrete, sell your body, beg. He can't even imagine. But it doesn't change the fact that Wain has disappeared. That he has done so before. Presumably there's somewhere he goes, somewhere nobody knows about. Maybe he has a friend he stays with, a friend no one in his family has ever met.

"My sister Enid's home right now," Amie says. "I told her we'd come by. She works part-time at a drop-in center for kids, so she might know someone who's seen Wain."

She tosses her cup in the recycling bin and waits for Sid to do the same. He follows her down an alley and up a steep set of stairs in an old building that smells of cat piss and garbage. When they knock on the door of the apartment at the head of the stairs, it's opened by what appears to be a geisha.

"Hey, Enid," Amie says. "Cool kimono."

Enid bows and murmurs, "*Konnichiwa*," and steps aside to let them enter the tiny apartment. She is wearing white socks with black flip-flops, and her black wig is askew.

"Enid's in the theater program at the university. They're putting on *The Mikado*," Amie says to Sid. "She's a Method actor. Obviously."

Enid pulls off the wig and puts it on the futon beside her; it looks like a black spaniel puppy. Her blond hair is French-braided close to her head. "That thing makes my head soooooo itchy," she says, "especially under the lights."

She sticks her hand out at Sid. "You must be Sid. I'm Enid, otherwise known as Yum-Yum."

Sid sings a few bars of "Three Little Maids from School" and Enid's eyes widen. She clutches Amie's arm.

"Where did you find this delicious boy?" she says.

Amie rolls her eyes. "Ignore her, Sid. She's such a drama queen."

"But seriously, Sid darling, where did you learn to sing?" Enid takes off her kimono to reveal torn jean shorts and a brown short sleeve shirt with the name *Larry* embroidered on the breast pocket.

"At home," Sid answers. "Lots of Gilbert and Sullivan freaks on the island. Once a year we have a community sing-along. You pick stuff up."

Enid gives him an appraising look. "And they grow cherubim there too, I see." Her eyes, the light golden brown of pancake syrup, are amused, but kind.

"Cherubim?" he asks.

She frowns. "No, that's not right. You look like a Caravaggio cupid. The eyes, the curls, the lips. Innocence wronged." She turns to Amie. "Am I right?"

"Art history class," Amie says to Sid. "Pay no attention. Show her the picture, Sid."

Sid pulls a picture out of his pack and hands it to Enid, who stares at it for a long moment before putting it down on a coffee table covered with musical scores and dirty dishes.

"The Green Knight," she says. "He's missing?"

No Such Luck

"You know him?"

Enid nods. "He comes in to the center sometimes."

"But he's not a street kid," Sid says. "Not really. He lives with his mom in Oak Bay. At least he did until a week ago."

"We don't ask too many questions," Enid says. "If a kid wants to talk, that's great. We've got a whole team of people—nurses, counselors, even a couple of lawyers who work for free. Most of the time, kids come in for a shower and a meal and somewhere safe to relax for a while. The Green Knight never said much. I never even knew his real name or how old he is."

"It's Wain—Gawain, actually. And he's thirteen."

"Thirteen. I would have said fifteen, at least. And his mom is…where?"

"She took off a couple of weeks ago," Sid says. "She's bipolar. Off her meds."

"Are you close to your mom?"

Sid ponders the question for a moment before replying. He's not sure how much of his history he wants to reveal to her—a complete stranger. This isn't about him anyway—it's about Wain.

"No," he says. "I'm not close to my birth mother." When Enid raises an eyebrow at him, he adds, "I've been living with my parents—my foster parents—since I was two. I'm real close to them. I never even knew Wain existed until a few days ago."

"And you came looking for him?"

Sid nods. "It seemed like the right thing to do. I have a grandmother too. Elizabeth. I wanted to meet her."

Enid gets up off the futon and hoists an enormous satchel over one shoulder. She looks like a hipster Mary Poppins. She could have anything in that bag: a lava lamp, a bottle of Jägermeister, a Bowie knife, a wedding dress, a six-course meal.

"Let's go then," she says. Sid and Amie follow her out the door and down the filthy stairs.

"Where are we going?" Amie asks.

"To the center. Maybe someone else has seen him. You got more of those pictures?" she asks Sid.

Sid hands her half a dozen photos, which she stuffs into the giant bag.

Enid moves like a race walker—arms pumping, hips swiveling, sandals slapping the pavement, heel, toe, heel, toe—and Sid has to almost run to keep up. Soon they are in a part of the harbor Sid hasn't yet explored, where the buildings are more industrial, less tarted up for tourists. They pass a shelter where a group of men have congregated on the sidewalk, smoking and panhandling. A couple of them greet Enid, and she hands them Wain's picture and asks them to look for him.

"Sure thing, Enid," they say. "We'll keep an eye out."

"He looks real young," a toothless man with long filthy gray hair says. "Too young for this life."

Enid nods and puts her hand on the man's sleeve. "You're right, Milo. He looks older than he is. So if you see him, don't spook him. Just call me at the center, okay? Or call the number on the back of the picture." She hands him a business card, which he stuffs into his jacket pocket.

"Will do, Enid," he says.

As they walk away, Enid asks Sid how old he thinks Milo is.

"Seventy?" Sid suggests.

"He's forty-five," Enid replies. "Been on the street for years. Used to be a stockbroker. Got into cocaine. Lost everything. Started smoking crack and drinking a lot. He's a good guy though. Looks out for the younger kids. Sends them to the center."

Sid doesn't know what to say. Enid was right—he is an innocent. What else did she call him? A cherubim?

He isn't sure what that is, exactly—something to do with angels. He'll have to find out. All he knows is that he is out of his element here, although he's not as anxious as he expected to be. More like unnerved. Nothing he has experienced on the island has prepared him for any of this. He feels like apologizing for his innocence, his stupidity, his ignorance, although he knows it's hardly his fault. Enid and Amie swerve suddenly into a small brick building, and Sid almost misses the turn. A hand-painted sign above the door says *StreetSafe Center*. On the dirty wall inside the door is another sign: *If you're high or holding, come back when you're not.*

Enid waves at a woman sitting at a desk in the hallway.

"Back so soon?" the woman says.

"Yeah. Can't stay away." Enid laughs. "This is Sid. His brother's missing. The Green Knight. You remember him?"

"Sure," the woman says. "Hard to forget the Green Knight. How long has he been missing?"

"About a week," Enid says.

The woman frowns. "Where's his mom and dad?"

"His mom's AWOL," Enid says. "No dad. Can you ask around, put up his picture?"

"Sure thing," the woman says. "I'll call you if I hear anything. Good luck."

"Thanks, Barb," Enid says.

Amie and Enid chatter as they all walk back toward downtown. So and so is an asshole, *The Mikado*'s costume is too small, the guy playing Nanki-Poo is hot, gargling with salt water helps a sore throat, the wrap party is going to be at a wicked club. Sid lets their words wash over him—a wave of meaningless, harmless sound. He realizes how much he misses Chloe's babble, although he often tunes her out too. As they near the blue bridge, Sid makes a sudden decision to go to Elizabeth's. Even if she isn't home, he can sit in the sun by the walkway for a while.

"I'm going this way," he says, pointing across the bridge.

"Not for a while you're not," Amie says.

"What?" Sid hasn't expected resistance. After all, he's been with Amie and Enid for hours. They must have other, more interesting, things to do than hang out with him.

"Watch," Amie says as the bridge deck slowly lifts to allow a sailboat to pass underneath it. "Awesome, right? I never get tired of watching it. You'll be stuck here for a while though. It's not exactly fast."

Sid nods as the bridge finishes its slow ascent. He's not in a rush.

"Call me if you hear anything," Amie says.

Enid is already striding across the street. "You coming, Amie?" she yells.

"See ya, Sid," Amie says. "Gotta run. I'm helping out at the theater tonight. Dress rehearsal. I'm doing hair and makeup. It's not exactly a high-budget production. But you should come. You and your grandma. I'll text you the info."

"Sounds good," Sid says as she runs after Enid. He waits for the bridge deck to come back down and then he heads across, just as a tugboat passes underneath. A man in a yellow jacket looks up from the tug's deck and waves at him. Sid waves back and continues across the bridge. When he gets to Elizabeth's condo, there is no one home, so he finds a bench and gets out his sketchbook and colored pens. He wants to record everything he has seen today: Enid in her geisha costume, Milo's battered face, the sign at the drop-in center, the sailboat gliding under the raised bridge. He is so intent on his work that he jumps when he hears his name. Elizabeth is standing in front of him, a full bag of groceries in each hand.

"Want to do your good deed for the day?" she asks.

He leaps up, knocking his sketchbook and pens to the ground. He scrambles to pick them up; then he stuffs them in his backpack and takes the bags from Elizabeth.

She rolls her shoulders and sighs. "I always swear I'm only going for a few things and then"—she gestures at the bags—"this is what happens. Something's on sale, something else looks too delicious to pass up. What can you do?"

The handles of the cloth bags cut into Sid's palms. "How far away is the store?" he asks.

"Oh, a mile or so," Elizabeth says. "Not far. Taking the car is too much bother. And I need the exercise."

She opens the front door of the condo building, and they ride the elevator in silence. As they unpack the groceries, Elizabeth asks, "Any progress?"

"Sort of," Sid replies. He tells her about Enid and the drop-in center.

"That's good, dear," Elizabeth says. She sounds exhausted, but Sid can't tell if it's from her shopping expedition or from her family situation. Probably both.

"I can make tea, if you like," Sid says. "I'm good at it."

"I'm sure you are, dear," Elizabeth says. "That would be lovely. I'll just go put my old feet up, if you don't mind. The tea things are in that cupboard, and the kettle's on the stove."

When Sid comes into the living room with the tea tray, Elizabeth is stretched out on the red couch, swaddled in a plaid mohair blanket. Sid pours her a cup of tea—milk in first, please—and hands it to her. Her hand shakes slightly as she raises the cup to her lips.

"What were you drawing?" she asks. "I'd love to see."

Sid squirms. He's not comfortable talking about his drawing, let alone showing it to people. But it would be rude not to tell her something.

"Just some stuff I saw today: an old man who wasn't old at all; a geisha who wasn't Japanese. That kind of thing."

Elizabeth laughs. "Things that are not what they appear to be then."

"I guess so."

When he doesn't elaborate, Elizabeth says, "I guess you've been to Ripple Rock."

"Ripple Rock?" He's not sure why Elizabeth is asking about Ripple Rock, but he's grateful that she's changed the subject.

"Isn't it near where you live?"

"Kind of," Sid says. "It got blown up a long time ago though."

Elizabeth pulls herself up on the couch. "I know. I was at nursing school. When I heard they were going to blow an underwater mountain to smithereens, I was sure that a tidal wave as high as the Empire State Building was going to roar down Johnston Strait and sweep Victoria off the map. I rode my bike to the top of Mount Tolmie on the morning of the blast. I couldn't understand why no one else seemed concerned. Uniformed nurses were standing by to treat the injured in Campbell River, for heaven's sake. In my mind, the tidal wave looked like the wave in that famous Hokusai print—menacing but beautiful. But there was nothing for the nurses to do. According to the naturalists' reports, the blast barely disturbed the sea creatures in the area. So I've always wondered—what's Ripple Rock like now?"

Sid thinks for a minute before answering. Caleb loves to talk about Ripple Rock. One of his biggest regrets is that he was a baby when the explosion took place. He never got to see the murderous power of the rock.

"Whenever we go through the Narrows, Caleb always says, *He's still down there*, like the rock's a giant or a monster, but, to be honest, there's not much to see. It's way below the surface now, even at low tide."

Elizabeth sighs. "Even so, I'd love to see it. And to see where Devi lived and where you grew up. It sounds so...serene."

"Except for the occasional gigantic explosion," Sid says.

They sit quietly for a few minutes, watching a tiny yellow and green harbor-ferry pick up passengers at the hotel dock.

"Tell me about Wain," Sid finally says. "It's weird—I'm looking for him, but I have no idea what he's like, other than he likes to ride BMX and he's been getting in trouble lately. It's really hard to figure out where he might go."

"You're right, of course," Elizabeth says, holding out her cup for more tea. "Needle in a haystack. It might help if you knew whether you were looking for a knitting needle or a sewing needle or a hypodermic needle." She shudders. "Not that I think he's involved in the drug scene."

"Or with those scary knitters," Sid says with a smile.

Elizabeth laughs and almost spills her tea. "You're a sly one, aren't you, Sid?" she says. "Wain's a bit like that: funny without being a clown. Although I have to say, he's much more extroverted than you."

"Almost everyone is," Sid says.

"Wain was such a lovely little boy. Happy, smart, friendly. Brave to the point of being foolhardy."

"So what happened?"

"Who knows? Puberty? His mother's problems? His father's absence? Hanging out with a bad crowd? One day he was a carefree child, rowing Stan's dinghy in the bay, memorizing the scientific names of sea creatures—I remember he always giggled when he said the word *nudibranch*. Then all of a sudden he was sullen and secretive and rude. Although I'm sure it wasn't sudden. None of us were paying close enough attention, I suppose. He first ran away when he was ten."

"Where did he go?" Sid asks, leaning forward in his chair.

"We never found out. He came back the next day. Hungry and very out of sorts."

"Did you call the police?"

Elizabeth shakes her head. "Devi didn't want to. She said she trusted him—a ten-year-old child! We had a big argument—didn't talk until the next time he took off. She called me to ask if he'd come to my house. I told her again to call the police. Phil told her the same thing. But by the time she called, he had turned up. That happened a few more times. Always the same thing: he and Devi have a fight, he disappears overnight and comes back the next day."

"But this is the longest he's been gone?"

"Yes. By far."

"So what's different?"

Elizabeth doesn't have to think very long. "Devi. Devi went off her meds. Trashed their house. He's never seen her like that—out of control. Violent."

"Violent?" Sid asks.

Elizabeth's face is ashen. Sid wonders if this is the first time she's considered that Devi may have hurt Wain.

He wishes he could reassure her, but he has seen too many abused kids come and go at home. Parental abuse is as common as dirt, Megan says.

"So he's probably gone where he always goes," Sid says slowly. "He's just staying away longer because he's afraid to come home."

"But he must know how worried we are. And Devi hasn't come back."

"But he doesn't know that, does he?"

"I suppose not."

"So we have to find him and tell him," Sid says, although he has no clear idea how this will happen. He puts the teacups back on the tray and takes the tray into the kitchen.

"Just leave the dishes," Elizabeth calls from the living room. "I'll take care of them later."

"I got it," Sid says, nestling the cups into the top rack of the dishwasher. It's a familiar task, and it calms him.

When he goes back into the living room to say goodbye, Elizabeth is asleep, so he leaves her a note on a page torn from his sketchbook: *Gone back to Phil's. See you tomorrow?* He signs it with a tiny drawing of himself riding across the bridge on Wain's bike. Blue bridge, green bike, red hair, yellow sun.

What the Fuck

For the next few days, Sid follows the plan: papering downtown with Wain's picture, sometimes with Amie, sometimes alone. At night he stays home and draws or watches TV while Phil drives around downtown, talking to hookers and cops and drug dealers. No one has seen Wain.

One morning, after almost a week in Victoria, Sid wakes up in Phil's loft, a cat on his head, another on his feet. He looks up at the cloudless sky. It's a beautiful day and he can't bear to go back downtown. Besides, he's had an idea that's worth exploring, although he's not ready to share it with anyone yet. First he has to call Megan.

When she answers, he updates her on the search for Wain and reassures her that he is all right.

"You have a friend down here, right?" he asks. "Wanda? Wendy? The one with the sailboat. Do you know where she keeps her boat?"

"Wendy," Megan says. "As far as I know her boat's still in Oak Bay Marina. Why?"

"I thought I'd go visit her," Sid says. "What's the name of her boat again?"

"*Delirious.* Shouldn't be hard to find. Just ask for the crazy lady with the purple boat." Megan laughs. "Tell her I said hi. Ask her to stop in if she's ever up this way."

"Okay. Gotta go. I'll call later, maybe talk to Fariza."

"I miss you, Sid. We all do."

"Miss you too," Sid says. "Bye."

After breakfast he says goodbye to Phil, who is ankle-deep in sawdust, and walks down to the marina where the cement killer whale guards the parking lot. Phil told him that there used to be an aquarium next to the marina, with live killer-whale shows and seals that took showers and "talked" to the tourists. You could even brush the whales' teeth. It makes Sid feel sick just to think about it. Seeing orcas in the wild always brings tears to his eyes: the grace, the power, the sense of community. If he wasn't in a human family, he would want to be a calf in a killer-whale pod. He climbs up next to the orca and rubs its rough cement side. "Wish me luck," he says under his breath.

He scrambles down and strolls to the small park that overlooks the marina. He's stopped here a few times before. There is an old-fashioned wooden double swing near the pebble beach, the kind where you sit facing someone else and push on the floor to make the swing move. Sid stands on the center of the swing and sways back and forth until the swing starts to follow his movement. He scans the marina for a purple boat, but he's too far away to see all the docks. But he can see the small island that seems to sit within walking distance of the last jetty. A stone's throw away. Of course, it's an illusion; the island's not that close, but it's close enough. Just like the island in the cove near his house. The one he always went to when he wanted to be alone. The island Caleb always rescued him from.

He jumps off the swing and walks through the parking lot to the marina, where he methodically walks up and down each dock, looking for *Delirious*. He supposes he could ask at the office, but he's enjoying being on the dock. When he was small, he used to tell everyone he was going to be a wharfinger when he grew up—he loved both the word and the idea of running a wharf. He wonders if the word is even used anymore. When he finally finds the purple ketch, he's on one of the farthest docks. A woman with very short gray hair is sitting in the cockpit, polishing one of the many brass fittings.

"Wendy?" Sid says.

She looks up, her leopard-print half-glasses crooked on her nose.

"Who wants to know?" She's smiling when she says it, and Sid smiles back.

"I'm Sid, Megan and Caleb's kid. From the *Caprice*?"

Wendy puts down her polishing rag and stands up. She is very short and very round, but she leaps out of the cockpit as nimbly as a teenager.

"Little Sid," she says. "I should have known. That hair! Come aboard. Come aboard. Is the *Caprice* here? Tell me everything."

"Nothing much to tell," he says when they are settled in the cockpit and Wendy has resumed polishing. "I'm here on my own. I could use your help though."

"My help?" Wendy keeps polishing, but Sid knows she's paying attention. For some reason, it's easy to tell her about Devi and Wain. When he shows her Wain's picture, she gasps and puts her hand to her enormous chest.

"*That's* your brother?" she says. "He's here all the time. Hanging around, trying to get people to take him out on their boats. Most of us just shoo him away like a harmless bug. How long did you say he's been gone?"

"Almost two weeks now," Sid replies.

"And you think he might be over there." She points at the island.

Sid nods. "That's where I would go if I wanted to run away. All he would need is a dinghy. Maybe he stole one. Dragged it out of sight when he got there."

"And you want to row over to Jimmy Chicken and see if you're right?"

"To where?"

"To the island. Locals call it Jimmy Chicken Island, after the old Native man who used to live there years ago."

Sid nods. "I don't know where else to look."

"Well, thank you for not stealing my dinghy," Wendy says. She scuttles down into the cabin and comes back up with two chocolate bars and a can of Coke. "If he's there, he'll be hungry. Do you want company?"

Sid imagines the two of them in the small rowboat. She must weigh close to 200 pounds. "I think it's better if I go alone. If that's okay."

"Fine by me," Wendy says. "Two things though. Wear a life jacket and take one for Wain. Megan would kill me if anything happened to you."

It seems like a small price to pay, even though the life jackets are ancient, bulky and moldy.

"Land on that little beach at the southern tip; everywhere else is too rocky. And if you get into trouble, call me on my cell—the service is great here." She pulls a pen out of her pants pocket and writes a number on the back of one of the chocolate bars. "If you can't bring him back yourself, we can call for backup."

"If he's there at all," Sid says.

"Well, you won't know if you don't row." Wendy unties the ropes holding the dinghy and steadies it while Sid climbs in. "Good luck," she says as she pushes him away from the wharf.

The water is calm and Sid is a strong rower; he is on the island in less than ten minutes. As he pulls the dinghy up onto the beach and secures it to a log, a flock of geese rises from the rocks and flies out across the bay, honking its displeasure at being disturbed. There is goose shit everywhere. And no sign of another dinghy.

The shoreline is rocky and ringed with prickly bushes: gorse and wild rose. Just past the little beach is a path that leads around the tip of the island and through a tiny meadow, the size of a king-size quilt. He walks toward the center of the island, being careful to avoid the goose shit. He turns to look north, toward home, and stumbles over what he first thinks is a snake and then realizes is a coiled rope. A rope attached to a dinghy. A dinghy camouflaged with branches to form a small cave. Sid is crouching to peer inside when he is flattened from behind by what feels like a wild animal. A large dog, a wolf, a cougar. He knows this is crazy, especially since his assailant is swearing loudly as he flails at Sid. A few blows land on Sid's back before he's able to throw whoever it is off.

"Get away from my boat!" his attacker screams, punching the air near Sid's head.

Out of the corner of his eye, Sid sees a black fist and arm. "Wain!" Sid yells. "Wain, stop it." The flurry of blows slows down, and Sid is able to turn around.

"How do you know my name?" Wain snarls. "Who the fuck are you? What do you want?" He staggers away from Sid and collapses onto a lichen-covered rock, his chest heaving. He is way bigger than Sid, but his bulk seems soft, almost flabby, and he is sweating heavily. Sid is surprised he was able to land even a single blow.

"Do you want something to eat?" Sid asks. "I've got chocolate. And Coke." One thing he's learned from watching Megan deal with sad, angry, uncommunicative kids is to offer food and drink first. Before anything else. Hunger and thirst are two demons that can be easily placated.

Wain eyes him suspiciously as Sid tosses him a chocolate bar and the Coke. They sit in silence as Wain, who is still breathing hard, eats and drinks. When he is done, he throws the wrapper and the can into the bushes. Sid decides not to play park warden. He can pick up the trash later.

"Who the fuck are you?" Wain repeats.

Sid clears his throat. Now that the moment has come, he wants to lie and say, "I'm Phil's nephew." Instead, he takes a deep breath and says, "My name's Sid. I'm, uh, your brother. Half brother, actually."

"No fuckin' way." Wain glares at him. "I don't have a brother. Mom would have told me."

Sid shrugs. "You sure about that?"

Wain's eyes widen and then he looks away. "She took off," he says. "She back yet?"

Sid shakes his head. "I met Elizabeth though. She's worried about you. So's Phil."

"Why aren't they here then?" Wain asks. "I don't even know you."

"And I don't know you either," Sid says. "So we're even. I just wanted to find you, that's all. Phil's been looking all over for you. And Elizabeth's an old lady. They don't even know I'm here. You can do whatever you like—I'll be heading home soon. But I had to be sure you were okay."

"I don't need your help," Wain mutters, although Sid can see that his clothes are filthy and he can't stop shaking. "And I still don't think you're my brother. I mean, look at us."

Sid shrugs. "Genetics are a bitch. When your mom comes back, you can ask her. But you can't stay here forever. You're gonna run out of food. And, man, you really need a shower."

Wain raises one arm and smells his armpit. He recoils in disgust—an exaggerated movement that makes Sid laugh.

"Elizabeth told me you were a funny kid."

"She did?"

"Yeah. She told me lots of stuff about you—how smart you are, how brave."

Wain ducks his head. His tightly curled hair is full of dirt and debris. Sid stands up and looks toward the snow-capped mountain in the distance. He isn't sure, but he thinks Wain might be crying.

"What's that mountain called again?" Sid asks.

"Mount Baker," Wain says, his voice muffled.

"Ever been there?" Sid asks.

Wain snorts. "Do I look like I ski? Too expensive. And it's not even in Canada. You need a passport."

"Right. So, you gonna come back with me?"

"Now?" Wain jumps up and backs away as if he thinks Sid is going to tackle him.

"Yeah, now. I borrowed a dinghy. I gotta get it back.

"I stole mine," Wain says. "Only pussies borrow things."

"Well, I'm a pussy then. But I have to take mine back. And then I have to tell a bunch of people that I found you. Enid, Amie, Phil, Elizabeth. So any way you look at it, you're coming back. We can row back together. Or the police can come and drag you back."

"Fucking pigs," Wain says. Then, "You know Enid?"

"Yup. She's goin' nuts worrying about you." This is an exaggeration, but Sid knows Enid won't mind. "She's got that show and she's been missing rehearsals to search for you."

"She has?"

Sid nods. "What else you got here?" He walks over to the dinghy and turns it over—a dirty down sleeping bag and a pillow, as well as some bottled water and a box of crackers. "That what you've been living on?"

"Yeah." Wain starts throwing everything into the dinghy. "The worst thing is hanging your ass over the water to take a shit. It freezes your balls off."

"I bet," Sid says as he retrieves the candy wrapper and the Coke can and they carry the dinghy to the little beach.

Wain laughs when he sees the purple dinghy. "You borrowed Crazy Wendy's boat?"

"She's a friend of my mom's. She was cool about it."

"Your mom?"

"The woman who raised me. Megan. She's my mom."

Wain slides his dinghy into the water and jumps in.

"Race you, pussy," he yells at Sid, who scrambles to catch up. Even though Wain has a head start, Sid is lighter and a stronger rower. He reaches *Delirious* a minute or two before Wain. Neither of them are wearing their life jackets.

"Mission accomplished, I see," Wendy says to Sid as she watches Wain row alongside. "Mr. Manning will be glad to have his dinghy back. Use my hose to clean it off first."

"You gonna tell him?" Wain asks Wendy as he and Sid pull the dinghy up onto the wharf, empty it and hose it down.

"Should I?" she asks.

Wain looks at his shoes.

"Don't do it again," Wendy says. "If you need to borrow a dinghy, come and talk to me. You got it?"

Wain nods. He and Sid carry the dinghy back to the wharf beside *Hither and Yon*, the boat it belongs to. Luckily for Wain, there is no one aboard.

They walk back to Wain's house together, Sid carrying the pillow, Wain lugging the rolled-up sleeping bag. The closer they get to the house, the slower Wain walks. They are moving so slowly, an old woman with a walker passes them, muttering something about *boys these days*.

"How did you know where to look for me?" Wain asks.

"I didn't," Sid answers. "It was just a lucky guess. I was riding around looking for you, and I kept going by the marina. The island reminded me of a place I go to at home. And I figured that if you really didn't want to be found, you'd go somewhere where no one would see you. That's what I'd do."

"Were you riding my bike?" Wain doesn't seem annoyed, just interested.

"Yeah. I never left it unlocked anywhere or anything. It's a cool bike. Great name: The Green Knight."

"You know about the Green Knight?" Wain asks.

"Yup. And I know your name's Gawain."

"What's your name?"

"I told you—it's Sid."

"No way Devi named you plain old Sid. What's your real name?"

Sid laughs. "Ever read 'Rumpelstiltskin'?"

"Sid's short for Rumpelstiltskin? No way. That's wild, even for Devi." Wain stops on the sidewalk and stares at Sid. "I thought Gawain was bad. Sorry, man." He shakes his head sorrowfully. "Yours is way worse."

"My name's not Rumpelstiltskin," Sid says. "I was just thinking about the fairy tale—when the queen has three days to guess the dwarf's name. Maybe I should make you guess."

"And maybe I should kick your ass again," Wain says, punching Sid in the shoulder.

"Again?" Sid says, dancing out of reach of Wain's fists. "I'll tell you my name on one condition."

"What's that?"

"You stop hitting me."

Wain shrugs and ambles on. "Whatever. Okay."

They turn the corner onto Wain's street.

"Siddhartha," Sid says. "My name is Siddhartha Eikenboom. Named for the Buddha." He puts his palms together and bows deeply toward Wain. "Namaste, little brother."

"Fuck you," says Wain.

Not So Much

"I found him." Sid is in the loft at Phil's, under the duvet, talking to Megan on the phone. He has already left messages for Enid and Amie, who are probably at the theater. Phil and Wain are at Devi's house, waiting for Elizabeth. Sid has come back to the garage because he figures it's not really his family reunion, and besides that, he's exhausted. There's talk of going out for dinner, to celebrate, but he's not sure he'll go.

He tells Megan about the island, about borrowing Wendy's dinghy, about Wain's black fists pummeling his back.

"So you're a hero," she says.

Sid shrugs and then realizes she can't see him.

"How did you know where to look for him?" Megan asks.

"Just a lucky guess. No one had seen him downtown, at least not lately, so I thought about where I would go, and the island was so close, like the one in our cove."

"What's he like?" Megan asks.

Sid isn't sure how to answer, so he says the first thing that comes into his head. "He's really...black. Blacker than Fariza. Inky. But his eyes are just like mine. It's weird. Except for that, no one would ever guess we share any genetic material. He's tall—taller than me—and kinda thick, you know, but strong, I think. At least usually. He was pretty weak when I found him, but he put up a good fight. Not that I fought him, or anything," he hastens to say. "I just yelled at him to stop, and he did. Lucky for me, right?"

Megan laughs and Sid wishes he was sitting with her at the kitchen table, not lying in a stranger's loft, avoiding his new family.

"Do you want me to come and get you?" Megan asks.

Sid thinks for a minute before he answers. He's not sure yet how he feels about Wain—it doesn't seem fair to judge him on such a brief acquaintance—but he knows he likes Elizabeth. Maybe he should stay for a few days, spend some time with her. But what if Devi comes back? Sid shivers under the duvet, even though it's warm in the loft.

"I can take the bus back," he says. "I still have some money. And I think I want to stay for a bit. Is that okay?"

There's a small silence before Megan speaks, and Sid wonders if she wants to tell him to come home right away, not to get any more involved. Even if that's what she wants, all she says is, "Of course that's okay. They're family."

"No, they're not," he says.

"They are, Sid. Just a different one than you're accustomed to. It's going to take some getting used to. For all of us. Give it a bit of time."

"Don't you want me to come back?" The words are out of his mouth before he can stop them, even though a moment ago he had been worried that she might not want him to stay away. He hates the way he feels. His emotions are jagged, like the edge of one of Phil's saws. Useful if you know how to handle them. Sharp and dangerous if you don't.

Megan laughs. "Don't be ridiculous, Sid. Of course we want you back. This is your home. But if you want to stay down there for a bit, that's fine too."

"Maybe for a couple of days then," Sid says. "Is Fariza okay?"

"She's fine. Chloe comes over every day and they play what I used to call Beauty Parlor. They call it Day Spa. They've even done seaweed wraps on each other, which was pretty funny. And smelly. Hot stone therapy is next, apparently. Caleb and I are their test clients. Caleb said the mud mask was pretty awesome. Chloe's talking about making business cards, god help us."

Sid feels a twinge of what he thinks might be jealousy. He's never wanted a seaweed wrap—he doesn't even know what it is—and he knows if he was there, he'd stay as far away as possible from hot stone treatments and mud masks, but he doesn't want Chloe taking his place in Fariza's affections. It's not a noble thought, but it's still true.

As if he has spoken aloud, Megan says, "Don't worry. Fariza still spends hours every day writing in her sketchbook. She hasn't forgotten you."

"How can you tell?"

"When she sees the ferry come in, she rushes to the window and watches the foot passengers walk off. When she realizes you're not there, she grabs Fred and goes to her room for a while. Even when Chloe's here, they take ferry breaks. We keep telling her you'll be back, that we'll know which ferry you'll be on and we'll go down to meet you. But you can tell she's worried."

"Is she there?" Sid asks. "Can I talk to her?"

"Hang on, I'll get her."

Sid lies on his back and watches a helicopter pass overhead while he waits for Fariza to come on the line. He can hear Megan in the background, coaxing Fariza to pick up the phone. When he thinks he hears her breathing, he speaks. "Hey, Fariza, it's me, Sid. How's Fred? Megan tells me you're writing every day. And that you and Chloe have a spa. That's very cool. When I come back, maybe you can paint my toenails or something." Fariza giggles softly. Sid continues. "So I found my brother on a little island and brought him home. And I met my grandmother. Her name's Elizabeth. You might have seen her on TV. You'd like her, Fariza. I like her. Maybe she'll come and visit us sometime and you can wrap her in seaweed. I'm not going to be away much longer, I promise."

Sid hears someone come in downstairs. Phil's voice floats up to the loft.

"You awake, buddy?"

"Hang on, Fariza," Sid says. "I'm on the phone," he calls down to Phil. "Down in a sec."

"I'm just giving Elizabeth a few minutes alone with Wain," Phil says. "Then we're heading out for dinner. You up for that?"

Sid hesitates. He can hear Fariza hand the phone to Megan, who says, "You still there, Sid?"

"Yeah, I'm here. But I gotta go. I'll call you soon, okay." He shuts the phone after Megan says goodbye. He feels bad that he's cut the conversation short, but he's anxious to see Elizabeth again. He hopes Megan understands. If he's going to be presentable at dinner, he needs to have a shower. He's grubby from the trip to the island, and a bit sweaty from lying under the duvet in the late-afternoon heat. He grabs some clean clothes from his backpack and heads downstairs, where Phil is washing dishes.

"Do I have time for a shower?" Sid asks.

Phil nods. "A quick one." Sid disappears into the bathroom, where the sea monsters lurk. He runs a soapy hand over the tiles and the creatures undulate around him, alive but harmless.

Wain has the worst manners Sid has ever seen. The restaurant is Wain's choice, a chain that caters to young guys in expensive jeans with product-laden hair and girls in micro-minis and sparkly cleavage-baring tops. The wait staff—male and female alike—is uniformly attractive. The food is surprisingly good. When their entrees arrive, Wain attacks his with a gusto that turns Sid's stomach. He's sure Wain has eaten since their return from the island, but he still attacks his dinner like a wild animal, head down, arms protecting his plate from—what, predators? Maybe a few days without food will do that to you, but it's still gross. Unchewed food falls from Wain's mouth onto the table. Sid looks at Elizabeth, who raises her eyebrows at him and reaches over to touch Wain's elbow.

"Wain, dear, slow down," she says. "It's not a race."

Wain looks up at her and says, "You try eating crackers for a week."

Sid wants to knock Wain's plate to the floor and make him apologize to Elizabeth, but he knows he won't. For one thing, he's too tired to confront Wain; for another, it's not his job to discipline his little brother, although he knows what Caleb would have done: taken away the food and frog-marched Wain out of the restaurant. Phil and Elizabeth exchange a glance across the table, and Elizabeth shakes her head slightly. Not tonight, she seems to be saying. Phil returns to his bowl of pasta, Elizabeth picks at her salad and Sid takes a few bites of his halibut burger. It's good, but he's lost his appetite.

"You gonna eat that?" Wain points at Sid's plate.

"No."

"Can I have it?"

"Sure." Sid pushes the plate across to Wain, who shovels the food into his mouth, barely chewing it before he swallows. When the plate is empty, he belches loudly and grins. There is a piece of lettuce in his teeth.

Phil stands up, leaves a pile of bills on the table and helps Elizabeth to her feet. A middle-aged woman at the next table frowns at Wain as he walks by. He glares at her and says, "What are you lookin' at?"

"You gotta tone it down, buddy," Phil says to Wain as they leave the restaurant and walk to the car.

Sid snorts and Wain turns on him. "What's your problem, man?" He flicks Sid's curls with a large greasy finger.

"That's enough, Wain," Elizabeth says, her voice sharp and even. She links her arm in Sid's and they continue in silence to the car. Wain runs ahead of them, whacking each parking meter that he passes with an open palm. It must hurt, but he keeps it up for two blocks. When they get to Elizabeth's car, he is sitting cross-legged on the hood, listening to his iPod and singing along to some Kanye garbage. Sid hates Kanye.

No one speaks on the ride back to Phil's house. Wain is still plugged into his iPod, Elizabeth closes her eyes and rests her head against the window and Phil drives, his mouth clamped shut in a hard line. A muscle in his jaw twitches. When they get to Phil's, Elizabeth gets into the driver's seat as Wain disappears into Devi's house without a backward glance. Phil leans down and kisses Elizabeth on the cheek. Sid squats down to pet the cats, who always appear when a car pulls into the driveway.

"I'm sorry," Phil says. "I shouldn't have suggested going out."

"Not your fault," Elizabeth replies. "It's hard for Wain. People coming and going out of his life. Devi gone, Sid here." She looks at Sid. "I don't mean that you shouldn't have come, dear. It's just confusing. For everybody."

Sid nods and stands up, brushing the cat hair off his hands. He can't pet the cats for too long or his eyes start to itch. Thanks, Devi, he thinks.

"It's no excuse for rudeness, Elizabeth," Phil is saying.

"Ah, but it is," Elizabeth replies.

Phi shakes his head.

"Maybe not an excuse then," Elizabeth says. "A reason. A good reason."

Phil shrugs. "I don't know. I can't stand it when he behaves that way—like he's never been taught any manners. Like he's some kid from the projects, for chrissakes." He straightens up and slaps the top of the car, hard enough to leave a dent. "Let's talk soon," he says before he turns away and walks toward Devi's house. Sid is glad he is staying in the garage. He doesn't want to be around Wain right now, even though he does feel kind of sorry for him. But Phil is pissed, and Sid doubts whether he's going to make hot chocolate and read Wain a bedtime story.

Elizabeth turns to Sid. "Lunch tomorrow?" she asks.

"Sure," he says.

"He didn't come home last night." Sid can hear Phil talking on the phone downstairs. It's early—barely light— and there are still some stars visible through the skylight. Phil must be talking to Elizabeth, who is an early riser.

"I'm calling the police," Phil says. "This is bullshit. He's only been back three days and he's already pulling this kind of stunt. Yeah, I know he's unhappy, but he's not the only one." There is a pause, and then Phil says, "Okay, if he doesn't come back today, I'm calling the cops in the morning. And Social Services. Neither of us can take him on when he's like this. It's too much. For you, for me. The kid's got some problems—he needs more help than we can give. You know that." Phil ends the call with a promise to let Elizabeth know if Wain turns up.

Social Services, Sid thinks. Foster care. He doesn't care what Phil and Elizabeth say about Devi. She's still a shitty mother. Abandoning first Sid and now Wain. Letting them be looked after by other people. He doesn't care about her illness or her reasons for going off her meds. He deserved better. Wain deserves better. Sid was lucky Megan and Caleb wanted him. Lots of other kids aren't so lucky—he knows that. He's heard the horror stories: foster parents who are just in it for the money, who abuse the kids in their care. Is that what will happen to Wain?

Sid sits up in bed. His sketchbook is on the floor beside the bed. Elizabeth has taken him to a different place every day since he found Wain. Sid has sketched until his hand cramped and his eyes twitched. Wicker tables set for tea in a lush seaside garden. A square concrete WWII lookout with rickety wooden steps. First Nations canoes sliding across glassy water as the sun sets on a pebbled beach. Children climbing on a green sea monster and a giant red octopus. He draws Elizabeth sitting on the sea monster's tail, her hair whipped by the wind off the water. He hasn't thought of Billy in days. He's almost embarrassed when he recalls the hours and hours—a lifetime, it seems—drawing imaginary characters in an imaginary world, when there is so much material right in front of him. He has a sudden vivid image of Megan working in her garden—weeding the dahlia beds, picking runner beans, staking tomatoes. How could he not have wanted to draw her? Or Caleb on the *Caprice*? Or Chloe at the lake? Or Tobin playing the guitar? He is suddenly and violently homesick. He needs to go home. But he can't abandon Wain. There's only one solution he can think of: Wain will have to come home with him.

He gets out of bed, pulls on some shorts and scrambles down the ladder. He can hear the shower running as he makes some toast and pours a glass of juice. He is sitting at the table, reading one of Phil's woodworking magazines, when Phil comes out of the bathroom, wrapped only in a worn blue towel.

"You're up early," Phil says.

"I'm going home," Sid says. "When Wain comes back."

"Okay."

"I mean, he probably went to a friend's house or something. Maybe he just fell asleep."

"Maybe," Phil says as he measures coarsely ground coffee into a glass carafe. The smell is amazing, even though Sid hates the taste of coffee. When he was little, he used to stand over Megan's fresh mug of coffee, inhale deeply, and say, "I want to drink the smell." They all still say that when something smells particularly good—lilac blossoms, cinnamon buns, fresh sawdust, their neighbor Marly's baby (although that can go either way).

Sid stands up and goes to the sink with his dishes. With his back to Phil, he says, "I think Wain should come home with me."

"What?"

Sid turns around to face Phil. "I think Wain should come home with me. Until school starts anyway. Megan and Caleb will be cool with it. There's lots of room right now—just one other kid besides me. And Megan says Wain is family and family should—" He stops.

Maybe Megan was wrong. Maybe he was crazy to think he could help. He has a vision of Wain wringing Fred's long pink flamingo neck. He can hear Fariza wail.

"Should what?"

"Help each other, I guess. If they can. If Wain came with me, it would help Elizabeth, right? And maybe it would help Wain. It can't hurt."

Phil presses the plunger down on his coffee. "Wain's pretty messed up," he says.

Sid nods. "Yeah, I get that. If it doesn't work out, you can come and get him." He's already starting to regret suggesting that Wain come with him.

Phil pours a mug of coffee and sits down at the table. He looks tired—there are bags under his eyes that weren't there when Sid first met him.

"Let's see what Elizabeth says. And your parents. They may not want another juvenile delinquent on their hands."

Sid laughs. "Megan loves a challenge."

"Well, Wain's a challenge, all right. Big-time. You call your mom and I'll call Elizabeth. If he comes back, we should be ready to roll. Don't want to give him the opportunity to take off again."

"*When* he comes back, you mean." Sid dries his hands and picks up the phone.

"Ah, the eternal optimism of youth," Phil says.

Join the Club

"Want to see Devi's stuff?" Phil asks. He and Sid are sitting in the overgrown garden between the garage and the main house. It's midafternoon and there's still no sign of Wain. Sid has spent the morning sleeping and drawing while Phil sawed and sanded in his studio. Lunch was cream cheese on a stale bagel. A wrinkled peach. A glass of tap water. Sid wonders if he should offer to go grocery shopping. Or mow the lawn.

"Her stuff?" For a minute Sid isn't sure what Phil means. Why would he want to see anything of Devi's? He has no intention of getting to know her—he doesn't even want to meet her—and what would her stuff tell him about her anyway? That she likes bright colors? That she reads vampire novels? That she doesn't care if her dishes match?

"Her studio," Phil explains. "I thought you might like to see what she does in there."

Sid looks at Devi's house. The studio windows run the entire width of the back of the house. North facing. Perfect light. Despite himself, he is curious. And a little freaked out. He's thought about it a lot since he's been here, that artistic ability could be inherited. And so could craziness. Maybe they are one and the same. He shivers and says, "Okay." Devi is a stranger, he thinks. A stranger connected to me by a loop of DNA. Might as well check it out.

As they cross the back porch of Devi's house, Sid notices that Wain's bike is gone. He's not sure if this is a good sign or not. It probably means he hasn't gone back to Jimmy Chicken, but beyond that, Sid can only guess. Maybe Wain has sold his bike on the street and jumped on a bus for parts unknown. He looks older than thirteen. Would anyone stop him—a kid in the summer, taking a bus to visit his grandma in Alberta or Ontario? Except his grandma is here. That must count for something, even in Wain's messed-up head.

Phil leads him through the unlocked back door and into the studio.

"Guess she hasn't been in here for a while," Phil says. "Usually there's a work or two in progress."

Sid looks around. Everything—the long scarred wooden worktable, the jumble of tiler's tools, the jars of shells and stones and sea glass, the huge cork

board covered in layers of curling, yellowed sketches—
is shrouded in dust. The windows are so dirty they are
almost opaque. The light is sepia-toned, like an old
photograph. Sid walks over to the cork board and stares
at the drawings, which look as if they were done in India
ink with a nibbed pen. The lines are strong, almost
savage, and the paper is torn in places where the artist—
Devi—used too much pressure. He lifts the top drawing
to look at another, and then another. All the drawings are
of crows: crows in flight, crows in trees, crows on power
lines, crows fighting over garbage, dead crows on the
road, crows on picket fences, crows popping out of a pie,
crows dive-bombing a short woman with gray curls. Self-
Portrait with Crows, Sid thinks. Another version of this
drawing shows the same woman lying on the ground;
crows are pecking out her eyes, there is blood on the
ground. The woman is smiling. At the top of the drawing
are the words *My Murder by Crows*.

Sid's stomach churns and he looks away, but not
before he sees a scrap of monogrammed notepaper at the
top of the board. The gold-embossed initials are plain
but elegant. *E.E.* Elizabeth Eikenboom. The handwriting
below is angular and upright. "*Arrange whatever pieces
come your way. Virginia Woolf,*" Sid reads.

"Devi used that as the inspiration for one of her best
pieces." Sid jumps at the sound of Phil's voice. He has
forgotten Phil is in the room. He moves away from the

cork board and stands at the worktable. He doesn't want to think about crows, but there are two in the apple tree outside the window. Not fighting or pecking out anyone's eyes. Just sitting, probably thinking about how to achieve world domination.

"It's a cool quote," Sid says.

"She made the piece from Cowichan River stones. It weighs a ton. I framed it in cedar and helped her hang it over her bed. Elizabeth said it would kill her in an earthquake and Devi just laughed and said, 'That's the idea, Mom.'"

"River stones," Sid says. "Isn't that how Virginia Woolf killed herself? Filling her pockets with river stones?"

Phil nods. "I'm impressed. You know about Virginia Woolf?"

Sid shrugs. "Megan's book group had a Bloomsbury phase. I eavesdropped."

"You're a funny kid," Phil says. "Devi has a strange sense of humor too."

"I'll say," Sid replies, although he's tempted to tell Phil he's full of shit. You can't inherit a sense of humor. But he does see Devi's point. Killed by your own art. It is kind of funny.

"Most of the work she does now is on commission. Memorial stones. For gardens."

"Memorial stones?" Sid can't imagine what these might be. Surely people don't put mosaic tombstones in their gardens. Then again, some people keep their loved ones in decorative urns on the mantelpiece. Anything is possible when it comes to the dead.

Phil pulls a black binder off a shelf and opens it on the table. Sid leans over and looks at a page of photographs of tiled paving stones, none bigger than a couple of feet across. Each stone has the dead person's name and dates woven into a design made with stones, beach glass, shells, shards of glass tile, specks of gold and silver. The images— a stand of deep-purple hollyhocks, a sailboat with a rust-red sail, a black dog with a blue bandana around its neck, an ancient tree, an old green pickup truck, a pink bicycle with training wheels—are detailed and exquisite.

"They're meant to be outside—catching the light, withstanding rain and snow—but they're not meant to be walked on. Too delicate. Some people bury the ashes underneath. Devi always said she wished people would let her mix the 'cremains' with the grout, but she only ever did that with her dad's ashes." Phil sighs. "She always got way too involved. I told her it wasn't healthy—interviewing the clients about the deceased for hours, looking at old photos, watching videos, searching for the perfect image. Sometimes—if it was a dead child—she would spend days in here. Not eating, not sleeping. She had to get it right. And she did. She has—had—more work than she could handle. I had to call all her clients a while ago. Even before she took off, she wasn't working."

Sid closes the book. He feels as if he's suffocating—from the dust and from Devi and her ghosts. He strides out of the house and into the garage, scrambles up the loft ladder and throws himself facedown on the bed. Tomorrow he will go home, Wain or no Wain.

Sid wakes up to the sound of someone pounding on Phil's door. It's still light out. He guesses it must be about nine o'clock. He has a headache and he's hungry, but he isn't ready to face anyone: not Phil, not whoever is pounding on the door. He wouldn't mind seeing Elizabeth, but he doubts whether she's the source of the pounding. He stares up at the skylight and listens.

First Phil's footsteps, then the door opening.

"Jesus, Wain!" Phil says. "What happened to you?"

Another man's voice. "You Phileas Phine?"

Sid imagines Phil nodding.

"He says his mother's away. Is that right?" A female voice this time.

"Yes," Phil says. "She's, uh, out of town, officer."

Officer. So Wain has been returned by the cops. Sid slides off the bed and peers down the ladder into the room below. Two cops take up almost the whole small room. Wain is standing between them. There is an open cut under his right eye and his lower lip is swollen and bleeding.

He is holding his left arm close to his body and taking shallow breaths.

"He says you're his guardian, sir," the woman says. "Is that correct?"

"His guardian?" Phil sounds surprised, but he recovers quickly. "Yeah, I am. And his grandmother is here in town too. We're looking after him."

"You sure about that?" The male cop sounds a bit aggressive, as if he'd like to pick a fight with Phil. "He was downtown, hanging with some pretty rough guys. He got beat up when someone tried to steal his bike."

"Assholes," Wain mumbles. "I kicked their asses."

"Language," the woman says. "Mr. Phine, this isn't the first time we've picked Wain up."

"Pigs," Wain says.

The woman sighs. "If he gets into trouble again, he might end up in juvie. You don't want that, Wain. Really."

"Bitch," Wain says. Phil grabs him by his elbow— his left elbow—and Wain screams. A high-pitched, girly scream.

"Apologize to the officer, Wain," Phil says through gritted teeth. "Now."

"You're hurting me," Wain whines.

"Now, Wain," Phil repeats.

"Sorry," Wain whispers.

"Louder," Phil says. "She can't hear you."

"It's all right, sir," the woman cop says. "I've been called worse."

"It's not all right," Phil says. "Louder, Wain, or they can take you back and throw you in a cell."

"I'm sorry, okay? I'm sorry." Sid can tell Wain is almost in tears, but Phil is unmoved. He simply lets go of Wain's arm and shoves him into a chair.

"Thanks for bringing him home, officers," he says. "I'll take it from here."

"He may need a doctor," the woman says. "Might have some broken ribs."

Phil nods and repeats, "I'll take it from here."

The cops turn to leave and Wain gives them the finger. Only Sid sees.

When the cops have gone, Sid climbs down from the loft and sits opposite Wain at the table while Phil cleans his cuts, applies a couple of butterfly bandages to the gash under his eye and wraps his ribs in wide adhesive tape.

"No way we're spending the night at Emerg," Phil says. "Waste of time. These are all surface cuts, and the ribs? All they'll do is tape them anyway. I'm going to phone Elizabeth from Devi's house. You two okay here?"

Sid nods. "What happened to the Green Knight?" he asks after Phil leaves.

"Assholes took it," Wain says. His speech is slurring and his eyelids are fluttering. He's only thirteen, Sid thinks. A kid. A tired, angry, confused kid.

"The guy who beat you up?"

Wain nods and a tear falls on the tabletop. He scrubs at it with his sleeve. "Two guys."

"Harsh."

More tears.

"I had an idea," Sid says. "About you. And me."

Wain sniffles and wipes his nose on his sleeve, which Sid takes as encouragement. At least he hasn't told him to fuck off.

"You could come back to the island with me. Hang out with me and my friend Chloe. Megan and Caleb will be cool with it. We could do some biking, go to the lake, maybe go out on Caleb's boat…" His voice trails off.

"Sounds awesome."

Sid can't tell if Wain is being serious or sarcastic; his nose is too stuffed up.

"Maybe Elizabeth could come too," Sid says.

Wain nods and puts his head down on the table. "So tired, man."

Sid considers dragging Wain up into the loft, but decides instead to let him sleep in Phil's bed. He's not sure Wain can make it across the yard to his own room, and Sid doesn't want to go back inside Devi's house.

"Come on, buddy," Sid says, pulling on Wain's good arm. Wain stands and, leaning heavily on Sid, staggers into Phil's room and collapses onto the bed, pulling his knees to his chest and moaning. Sid pulls off his runners and covers him with a blanket. "Sleep tight," he says.

Wain whispers something as Sid shuts the door. It's either "Fuck you" or "Thank you."

Phil comes back while Sid is on the phone with Megan. He looks panicked when he doesn't see Wain but relaxes when Sid points to the closed bedroom door.

"Not sure exactly," Sid says to Megan. "Tomorrow sometime though. You sure it's okay?"

He watches Phil make tea as he listens to Megan tell him how glad she is that he's bringing Wain to the island. He hopes she feels the same after she meets him.

"I told Wain he could come home with me," Sid says after he gets off the phone. "Hope that was okay. And I let him sleep in your bed too. He was dead on his feet. I took his shoes off."

Phil smiles for the first time that evening. "You're a good kid, Sid."

"Do you think Elizabeth would like to come? To the island?" Sid asks. "Megan says she's welcome to stay as long as she likes."

Phil nods. "Elizabeth loves road trips. Loves to drive. But you can ask her yourself. She's on her way over. I'd like to go to the mainland to look for Devi—maybe she's gone back to her old stomping grounds in Vancouver."

"Do you think Elizabeth would stop at McDonald's on the way over and get me a burger?" Sid says. "I'm starving."

"Jesus, I'm sorry," says Phil. "One kid injured, the other hungry. Not much of a guardian, am I?" He dials Elizabeth's number and asks her to pick something up. When she arrives she has hamburgers, yam fries, two kinds of salad and blackberry pie—enough for all of them, including Wain. It's definitely not from McDonald's.

"I have friends in high places," is all she says when Sid asks where the food came from. The burger is the best he has ever had. The pie is amazing—almost as good as Megan's.

When he finishes the last bite of pie, Sid says, "Wain wants to come home with me." He pauses and adds, "Well, he didn't say he wouldn't. And Phil wants to go to Van to look for Devi. Anyway, I wondered if you'd like to come too. To the island, I mean. Megan says it's okay. And I'd like you to come." He stops. He's babbling, but Elizabeth is smiling.

"A road trip," she says, her eyes shining. "Now that's something I haven't done in a long time. And I want to see your island, so yes! I accept your invitation, kind sir. When do we go?"

"Tomorrow?" Sid says. "I told Megan we'd come tomorrow."

"Excellent plan," Elizabeth says. "We'll whisk Wain away before he has a chance to change his mind."

"Change my mind about what?" Wain is standing in the doorway to Phil's room. "You guys woke me up."

He looks so much like a sleepy toddler after a nap that Sid can't help but laugh. "Dude, you need a shower," he says. "Especially if we're gonna be in a car for six hours."

"What car?"

"Mine," Elizabeth says. "We're going on an adventure."

"Screw adventures," Wain says. "You got any food?" This time everybody laughs, even Wain, who gasps, "It kills, man," as he clutches his ribs.

When Pigs Fly

"I ain't goin'." Wain winces as he crosses his arms over his chest and glares at Phil, who is stuffing an enormous black duffel bag into the trunk of Elizabeth's Honda. A night's sleep has not improved Wain's mood. "What if Mom comes back and no one is here? Ever think of that, asshole?"

Phil nods. "Matter of fact, I did. Her friend Holly is staying here until I get back from Vancouver. If Devi turns up, she'll call me." He slams the trunk shut. "And I'll call you. Now, get in the car."

For a second, Sid thinks Wain is going to hit Phil, which would be interesting to watch, but very stupid. Wain may be bigger, but he's also hurt and Phil is way stronger. From where he is sitting in the front seat of Elizabeth's car, Sid can see Wain's right fist clench and hear the sharp intake of his breath. Sid leans his head back against the headrest and closes his eyes. He just wants to get going.

Elizabeth leans out the window and says, "Wain, we're waiting," and he wrenches open the back door and lands in the backseat with a thud and a groan.

"I need some painkillers," he says. "And not just that Ibuprofen shit."

Elizabeth turns around to face him. "Ibuprofen's all you're getting, Wain. And stop talking as if you were born in the ghetto. It shows a paucity of imagination."

"A paw-what?" Wain says, slamming the door and fastening his seatbelt, which makes him groan again.

"A paucity," Sid says. "A lack. A dearth. A scarcity. An insufficiency."

"I get it, dude," Wain says, kicking the back of Sid's seat with one of his enormous runners. "And I got a good imagination. Better than yours, you pussy."

"Language," Elizabeth says as she backs out of the driveway.

"Pussy ain't swearing," Wain mutters.

"Pussy *isn't* swearing, you mean," Sid says.

"Who are you? The grammar police?" Wain snorts and jams his earbuds in his ears. "Let me know when we get there," he says.

Sid wakes up as the car clunks over the ferry ramp. He has been asleep in the backseat since they left Nanaimo, where they had stopped for lunch at Tim Hortons. Wain had yelled "Shotgun!" when Sid came out of the restroom. Sid didn't mind; he was all out of conversation.

Elizabeth turns around and smiles at Sid after the car is parked.

"Shall we go upstairs?" she asks.

Sid rubs his eyes and yawns as the ferry pulls away from the dock and starts across the channel. Almost home, he thinks. Half an hour and I'll be there. Maybe Megan has made cookies.

"C'mon, man." Wain jumps out of the car and races to the stairs, almost knocking over a young woman whose backpack is almost as big as she is. To Sid's surprise, Wain stops, apologizes and shoulders the gigantic pack, wincing as the pack thuds against him. The girl follows him to the stairwell, dread-locks swinging. Sid opens the door for Elizabeth and takes her elbow as they cross the car deck. The tide is running, and the ferry bucks a bit in the chop. The last thing they need is for Elizabeth to fall and break a hip. When they get to the passenger lounge, there is no sign of Wain.

"Probably on the upper deck," Sid says. "Want me to look?"

"I'll go," Elizabeth says. "Stretch my legs a bit. It's been a long drive."

"You sure?" Sid says. "The stairs are kinda steep. And it's really windy up there."

Elizabeth laughs. "I'm the Gray Matter Granny, remember?" She pats his hand. "You worry too much."

Elizabeth and Wain come back to the passenger lounge just as the ferry begins its wide turn into the cove, and the red railings of the government wharf come into view. Elizabeth's hair has come loose from its bun, and Wain looks like what he is, or should be anyway: a thirteen-year-old kid on vacation with his grandma and his brother, not a junior gangbanger.

"I always thought it was a nice touch that government wharves looked so cheerful and welcoming," Elizabeth says. "They must be a lovely pick-me-up on a gray day."

Before Sid can reply, Wain says, "This is awesome, dude. We saw whales! Killer whales! And Elizabeth says your dad has a boat. D'you think he'd take us out? There's this giant rock under the water—or there was until they blew it up."

Sid looks at Elizabeth and smiles. "She told you about Ripple Rock, huh? I can show you the explosion online, if you like. It's pretty cool. And yeah, I'm sure Caleb—my dad—will take us out on the boat. As long as you follow his orders and wear a life jacket and the right shoes." He likes saying "dad" even though he always calls Caleb by his first name.

When they drive off the ferry, Megan, Chloe and Fariza are in the parking lot, waving and jumping up and down next to the *Caprice Charters* van. They must have been watching every ferry, trying to spot them.

It's like I've been away for years, Sid thinks, like the Prodigal Son. Maybe they'll have a big barbecue tonight—kill the fatted calf, twenty-first-century style. Except didn't the Prodigal Son's brother try to kill him or something? Sid puts the thought out of his mind as Elizabeth pulls into the parking lot, and Chloe yanks him out of the car and throws her arms around him.

"I missed you so much," she says into his hair.

"Me too," he mumbles. She's rocking him back and forth, her bare arms still clamped around his neck. Her breath smells like it always does, of Double Bubble and strawberry lip gloss. "But you're strangling me."

"You deserve it," she says as she steps away from him and extends her hand to Elizabeth.

"Elizabeth, this is my friend Chloe," Sid says. "And my mom, Megan."

Even as he says it, he sees Elizabeth flinch slightly. But she is my mom, he thinks. Devi isn't.

"Welcome," Megan says.

"And this is my brother Wain," Sid says as Wain climbs out of the car.

Chloe squeaks, "Hey." Obviously no one has told her that Wain is a brother in more than one sense of the word. Wain looks at her as if she is a cupcake—a delicious, sweet, pink-iced, two-bite cupcake—and he hasn't eaten in weeks.

Sid leans over and mutters, "Try not to drool, man," in Wain's ear.

Wain grins—his teeth are orthodontist-straight and blinding white—and says, "Hey, Chloe. Nice to meet you. And you too, Mrs…" His voice trails off.

"Just call me Megan," she says. "Everyone does. And this"—she reaches behind her to pull Fariza forward—"is Fariza."

Wain squats down until he is eye level with Fariza. "I like your hair," he says, reaching out to touch a green bead.

Fariza runs over to Sid and wraps her arms around his waist. Sid bends over to hug her.

"What's her problem?" Wain asks, standing up and glaring at Sid and Fariza.

"Long story," Sid says. "She's not too keen on guys."

"Seems to like you all right," Wain says. "But wait, I forgot, you're a puss—" He glances at Elizabeth, who is standing a few feet away at the head of the wharf, where Megan is pointing out the *Caprice*. Wain lowers his voice and says, "You're a fag."

Sid ignores him, but Chloe grabs Wain's arm and he yelps in pain.

"What did you say?"

"Nuthin'. I didn't say nuthin'."

I didn't say anything, Sid thinks. He wishes Wain would cut out the tough-guy act. Nobody's impressed, especially not Chloe.

"You better not have," Chloe says. "Or I'll kick your black ass."

Wain grins. "You and what army?" He shifts his weight from side to side and fakes a punch at her head with his free hand.

"It's okay, Chloe," Sid says. "Let it go. Wain's full of shit."

Chloe lets go of Wain's arm and turns to Sid. "You need to man up," she says. "Or I'll kick your skinny white ass too."

"That's what I came back for," Sid says. "I missed all the ass-kicking."

"Who you calling full of shit, man? And how come you get to say *shit*?" Wain rubs his arm where Chloe grabbed him.

Chloe smiles as Megan and Elizabeth join them again. "Sid's special," she says sweetly. "You have no idea. Welcome to my world."

Fariza loosens her grip on Sid, takes him by the hand and leads him to the van, where Fred is buckled into an infant car seat, his head flopping to one side.

"Okay if I ride back here?" Sid asks. "Chloe, you can go with Wain and Elizabeth—show them the way. Fariza and Fred and I have things to discuss."

"She's hot," Wain says. He is sitting on the single bed in the room Megan has prepared for him. Sid is putting clean towels on the dresser.

"Who? Chloe? Yeah, I guess."

"You guess? Are you blind?"

"Shut up, Wain," Sid says wearily. "Unpack your stuff and come down for tea. Don't forget to wash your hands first or Megan'll make you do it."

He turns to leave the room. "You got everything you need? The bathroom's next door." He looks over at Wain, who is staring down at the hooked rug. "You okay?"

Wain looks up. "Yeah. I'm good."

He looks as if he might cry, but Sid has no more energy for Wain's outbursts. Maybe Megan can figure out what's wrong with him.

"Come down when you're ready," Sid says. "Or not. Megan made cookies though. Wouldn't want you to miss out."

Waking up in his own bed the next morning is bliss. Even the knowledge that he is sharing his home with his angry black brother can't diminish the pleasure of hearing Megan grind coffee in the kitchen, watching the sun wash the walls of his room with light, smelling the bacon that must signal waffles, even though it's not Sunday. Wain hadn't come down for dinner the night before; Megan took him up a tray of food and stayed for a minute to make sure he was okay. Sid thinks he heard him get up to go to the bathroom, but it could have been Elizabeth too.

Everyone had gone to bed early, after a simple supper of pasta and salad. No fatted calf. No murderous brother.

Not so far anyway. Sid had been glad of the dark and the silence broken only by the occasional cricket chirp and the sound of the toilet flushing down the hall. Now he hears Caleb's slow deep voice, and then Wain's, higher and faster. He rolls over and tries to prepare himself for another day with his brother.

Maybe Chloe will come over and mesmerize him with her crocheted bikini. Maybe Caleb will take him out on the boat. Maybe Megan will put him to work in the garden. Anything for a little peace and quiet, Sid thinks. He wants to sit at the table with Fariza, check out Eric the Eagle, watch the ferry lineup. He wants to see what Fariza has written; he wants to draw her story for her. Maybe he should start a new one of his own: *The Mighty Misadventures of Sid and Wain*. He smiles to himself as he pulls on some clean cutoffs and slides his feet into his Vans. He sniffs his pits and pulls a fresh T-shirt out of the drawer. There is a soft knock at his door.

"Just a minute," he says, his head stuck in the shirt.

The door opens a crack. A voice, soft as the dust on a moth's wing, wafts through the crack of the door and lands on Sid's shirt-shrouded ear. "Breakfast is ready."

"Fariza?" Sid says when he gets his head free of the shirt. "Fariza, is that you?" He wrenches the door open and runs down the hall. No Fariza. The door to her room is shut. He knocks. No answer. The toilet flushes and he can hear the water running. The bathroom door opens and Fariza comes out, wearing canary-yellow tights, a blue Canucks hockey jersey that comes to her knees, and UGGs that he thinks used to belong to Chloe. She holds up her hands to him, palms up, and smiles.

"Good girl," he says, "and thanks for calling me for breakfast. Wouldn't want to miss the waffles." He squats down so she can climb on his back, and he piggybacks her down the stairs and into the kitchen. As she climbs into her chair and settles Fred next to her, she looks up at Sid and places a finger to her lips. He nods and sits down next to her. If she wants to keep it a secret that she said something other than please and thank you, he's okay with that. For now, he's happy to think of those three little words—*Breakfast is ready*—as the perfect welcome-home present.

Go to Hell

"What happened to her?" Wain says. He is rinsing the breakfast dishes and Sid is loading them in the dishwasher.

"Don't know," Sid says.

"Must have been bad," Wain continues. "For her to stop speaking."

"I guess." Sid turns on the dishwasher. "She'll talk when she feels like it. And she always says please and thank you."

"Please and thank you," Wain repeats. "That's it? Weird."

"Yup."

"Does Megan know what happened to her?"

"Probably."

"Did you ask her?"

"No."

"But don't you want to know?"

Sid considers for a minute. When Fariza first came to the island, he was curious, so he understands Wain's interest. He chooses his words carefully. "Yeah, I'd like to know, but only if she wants to tell me, and only if it helps her."

"But she won't talk. So how can she tell you? And if it might help her to talk about it, why isn't Megan trying to get her to talk?"

Sid shrugs. "That's not the way Megan operates. She knows what she's doing. She says things happen when they're meant to happen. And you can't exactly make someone talk."

"But you would like to know?"

"Sure," Sid says, "if it would get you to shut up about it." He reaches out and gives Wain's shoulder a light shove, to let him know he's kidding. Sort of.

Fariza comes into the kitchen and drags Sid into the living room, where she has arranged the stuffies on the green couch. She points first at the couch and then at Wain, who is standing in the kitchen doorway.

"He might be a little old for that," Sid says.

"Old for what?" Wain asks.

"A stuffie. It's a house tradition. Every new kid gets to choose a stuffie. I still have mine. Spike. He's a porcupine. Fariza chose a flamingo."

"What am I, three?" Wain walks over to the couch and sweeps the stuffies off the couch; then he runs up the stairs and slams his bedroom door.

Fariza cowers behind Sid, tears in her eyes.

"It's okay, Fariza," he says. "Wain doesn't know he needs a stuffie. He's just really mad, but not at you. Or me." Is this what Devi is like when she's off her meds? He can't imagine what it would be like to be raised by someone whose moods were so erratic. The worst Megan ever did was swat him with a tea towel and tell him to shoo.

He shudders and puts his hand on Fariza's shoulder and steers her toward the big table. "Why don't you get your notebook and I'll get everything set up. You can show me your story. Okay?"

Fariza heads upstairs and Megan comes out of the War Room as Sid is lining up his pens and pencils on the table.

"Sorry about Wain," Sid says. "One minute he's okay; then he's freaking out."

"I'll talk to him later," Megan says. "When he's not feeling so out of sorts. Elizabeth is outside with her tea and a book. I've got work to do. Caleb says he'll show Wain the boat later. You and Fariza need some time together. She really missed you. She wrote in that book every day—wouldn't show it to anybody. Put it under her pillow every night."

Sid wants to tell Megan that he thinks Fariza might be starting to talk again, but before he can say anything, Fariza arrives back downstairs, notebook in one hand, Fred in the other. Fariza settles Fred in his chair and points out Eric, who is circling his aerie. The ravens on the wharf are so much more dignified than crows, Sid thinks. Ravens are magisterial. Crows are thugs. He pushes the image of Devi's self-portrait out of his mind as Fariza opens her notebook.

An hour later, he puts down his pens and flexes his fingers. "Time for a break, kiddo."

So far, the most interesting thing about what Fariza has written is her spelling. *Fred and I went to the store with Megan. We bott some flower and some butter and some choklit chipps. We helped Megan make cookies. Fred made a mess with the eggs. The cookies were reely good.* The next day, Fariza wrote: *I gave Fred a bath. Megan told me he was a water bird, but I think she is rong.*

Fariza smiles when she sees what Sid has drawn—Fred covered in raw eggs, Fred in the bath—but when he tries to look ahead in the notebook, she pulls it away from him, shuts it and runs upstairs. He puts away his stuff, pours himself a glass of juice and goes outside to find Elizabeth.

She is sitting on the porch, staring out at the cove.

"Is that where she tied up the boat? The *Amphitrite*?"

"I guess so," Sid says. "I don't remember the boat at all. Or her, really. I was only two." He feels a little mean, saying this, but he wants Elizabeth to understand: Megan is his mother.

"She sent me a drawing of the boat. She drew quite well, you know. Like you."

Sid shakes his head as if a wasp has landed in his hair. Not like him. Not at all.

"I would have come for you," Elizabeth says. "If I'd known. You must believe me. Stan and I..." She sounds as if she's about to cry, so Sid takes pity on her.

"I know. But Megan and Caleb—they took good care of me. The best. I'm sorry—"

She interrupts him. "Don't be. It's good to see you here—where you belong. I'm not saying anything should change, unless you want it to, of course."

Sid's not quite sure what she's talking about—he's had enough change recently to last him a while. He's saved from further conversation by Chloe's arrival with Irena, who is dressed to impress. She's wearing her Christmas dinner outfit: a pink Chanel suit, pumps, pearls. It looks insane on an August morning. Elizabeth, who has on pressed jeans, a crisp white shirt and black sandals, stands to meet her.

Chloe makes the introductions. "Mrs. Eikenboom, this is my grandmother, Mrs. Dawkins. Irena Dawkins."

"How very Dickensian," Elizabeth says. "Please call me Elizabeth."

"And you must call me Irena. And please—explain how my name is Dickensian. I don't remember anybody named Irena in Mr. Dickens's novels. And I have read them all." Irena lowers herself into a chair and waves regally for Elizabeth to sit again. "Is that tea? Sid, another cup please. Milk in first. And Chloe, a footstool perhaps?"

As Sid and Chloe leave the porch, they hear Elizabeth say, "Dawkins—it's the Artful Dodger's real name. And I only know because I have a friend who's mad for Dickens. Can't stand him myself. So sentimental."

"Do you think Irena will kill her?" Chloe whispers to Sid.

"Nah. Irena respects people who don't suck up to her. I never do, and she loves me."

Chloe snorts. "She loves you because you told her once she was the most beautiful girl in the world and you wanted to marry her. And yeah, I know, you were only five. But she's never forgotten. Wonder what she'll make of Wain. She wants you all to come for dinner soon. Roast beef, Yorkshire pudding. Trifle. The whole deal. It's like she thinks your grandmother's the Queen or something."

Your grandmother. It sounds so odd—as if he has suddenly acquired a third arm or a second head. Useful, but difficult to accommodate. He barely knows Megan's or Caleb's parents. Megan's mom died a long time ago and her dad married a woman Megan loathes. Caleb's parents still live in Newfoundland, where their "real" grandchildren are. Now Sid's "real" grandmother is sitting on the porch sipping tea.

Chloe picks up an old leather ottoman and heads back outside. "Hurry up with that tea, my good man. Spit spot." She giggles. "I feel like Mary Poppins. But cuter, don't you think?" She bats her eyes at Sid, who says, "I couldn't really say, m'lady."

"I brought my bike," Chloe says. "And my bathing suit. In case you want to go to the lake." Elizabeth and Irena have gone for a walk to see Irena's garden. No one else is around and lunch is hours away. If it was a normal day, Sid would help Megan around the house—water the garden, sweep the floor, scrub the bathroom, sort the laundry. But today doesn't feel like a normal day and all he can think of is the way the rocks by the lake heat up in the afternoon and how the lake water tastes like dead leaves, but in a good way. He wants to get away from Wain— at least for a few hours. Even Chloe's chatter seems soothing compared to Wain's mood swings. He knocks on the War Room door and Megan calls, "Come in."

He sticks his head into the room and says, "Me and Chloe are heading to the lake. We'll be back after lunch, okay? We're taking some food. Oh, and Irena has taken Elizabeth to see her garden."

"You got a bike I can ride?" Wain's voice rises up from the couch, where he has been invisible to Sid.

"A bike?"

"Yeah, so I can go the lake."

"You want to come to the lake."

"That's what I said." Wain sits up and Sid can see that his face is puffy. A pile of crumpled Kleenex lies on the floor by the couch. "I'm a good swimmer," Wain adds. "Faster than you, I bet."

"Is everything a competition with you?" Sid says, aware that an edge has crept into his voice.

"You can ride my bike," Megan says. "Caleb's will be too big for you."

"Is it pink?"

Megan laughs. "No, it's a regular old gray mountain bike. Not too embarrassing. Did you bring some shorts?" Wain nods, and she says, "Go get changed then. I'll pack you a lunch. Peanut-butter sandwich okay?" Wain nods again and leaves the room. Megan gets up and comes around the desk to Sid. "He's so lonely, Sid. And afraid. He needs to stay busy, keep his mind off his problems."

Me too, he wants to say, but Megan looks so worried he just shrugs and says, "Fine. But if he drowns, don't blame me. I'm not a lifeguard."

"Noted," Megan says. "Burgers for dinner? Chloe's welcome to stay."

"I'll ask her," Sid says. "And yeah, burgers would be good."

Wain rides ahead of Sid and Chloe all the way to the lake, calling back to them for directions. Sid is tempted to yell left when he should yell right, but he remembers the worry on Megan's face and sends Wain the right way. When Sid and Chloe get to the lake, Wain is already churning across to the far shore, his arms a blur. He is a powerful swimmer, even with his ribs taped.

Chloe squints into the sun. "Is he doing the butterfly?"

Sid shrugs and takes off his shirt. He swims well, but not particularly fast, and he has never mastered the butterfly. Not that he's wanted to. It seems so unnecessarily labor-intensive and show-offy. He wades slowly into the lake. Ankles, shins, thighs, crotch—pause—hips, waist, chest, neck, head. Before he gets fully submerged, Chloe races into the water with a *whoop*, diving as she runs and surfacing beside him to spit water in his face.

"Race you," she says.

He groans. "Not you too. Go and race Wain. I'm not into it today."

"Loser," Chloe says, spewing another mouthful of lake water at him.

He splashes her with the heel of his hand and she screeches and takes off across the lake. She does a pretty decent crawl, Sid thinks, but she'll never catch Wain.

He floats on his back, watching an eagle—maybe it's Eric—swoop into a cedar. He can hear splashing from the other side of the lake. Maybe Chloe has caught up with Wain. Maybe they'll leave him alone for a while. He does a lazy sidestroke toward an islet covered with gorse and scrubby trees, planning a circumnavigation.

When he is about halfway around the islet, a shriek pierces the silence. Chloe, her voice garbled, as if her mouth is full of water.

Sid flips over and does his best Australian crawl as fast as he can toward Chloe's voice. In the moments when his head is out of the water, he can hear Wain yelling, "Chloe! I didn't mean to!"

Sid is close enough now to see that Chloe is swimming toward him, flailing at the water like an out-of-control eggbeater. Wain is doing a slow breast-stroke behind her, groaning as he swims.

When Chloe reaches Sid, she grabs his arm and treads water. It takes a minute for him to realize that she is topless, and that Wain is holding her bikini top in his right hand.

"Give me that," Chloe yells. "And turn around—both of you."

Wain tosses her the scrap of fabric and she swims to the beach while the boys tread water, their backs to her as she pulls on her clothes. When she says it's okay, they swim to shore, and Wain staggers up the beach behind Sid, sputtering, "I didn't do anything...I didn't mean to..." The tape that was wrapping his ribs has slid down around his hips, like a wet diaper.

Chloe turns on him. Her hair is plastered to her face and she is shivering, but her fists are clenched, her body tensed as she leans toward him.

"Get away from me, you little perv," she yells.

Wain steps back and turns to Sid. "She's nuts, man. I didn't do anything. Her top came off..."

"Because you pulled it off, jerkwad. And then you had a good look," Chloe says. "You're lucky all I did was kick you in the balls."

"It was an accident," Wain says. "The bow just came undone."

"Shut up, Wain," Sid says. "And get lost. I mean it. Good luck finding your way home."

"I didn't hurt her, man."

"Shut up," Sid says again. Chloe is shaking now, her teeth chattering. Wain grabs Megan's bike and rides away, swearing as his crotch makes contact with the seat.

Sid sits on a rock and pulls Chloe down beside him. He rubs her back in small circles and she leans against him, her muscles gradually relaxing, her eyes closing.

Sid puts his arm around her and she nestles into his chest. He hopes she can't feel how fast his heart is beating.

They sit in silence for a long time before she speaks.

"That kid is super fucked up."

"I know," Sid says. "Believe me, I know."

"I should have drowned him."

"Probably not your best choice."

Chloe shrugs. "It's not that big a deal anyway. It's not like he touched me or anything. And I hurt him pretty bad. Don't tell anyone, okay?"

"What if he tries again?"

"He won't," Chloe says. "I'm gonna tell him that if he ever does anything like that again, I'll cut off his dick. Okay?"

"Okay," Sid says. "You're the boss."

"Anyway, he's your brother, Sid," Chloe says. "I don't want to get him in trouble."

"Half brother," Sid says as they climb on their bikes and head for home. "Only a half brother. And he's already in trouble."

Oh My God

"You coming in?" Sid asks when they stop at the end of his driveway.

Chloe shakes her head. "I don't want to see that little shit anytime soon. Besides, I need a shower. My hair's a disaster. Maybe I should cut it all off or put it in cornrows, like Fariza's. What do you think?" She pulls a strand of hair in front of her face and examines it closely, going a bit cross-eyed. "The ends are, like, totally split."

"I'm sorry," Sid says.

"For my split ends? Not sure how that can be your fault." She tucks her hair back behind her ears and smiles at Sid. Her lips are a bit cracked and the skin on her shoulders is peeling—not enough sunscreen—but otherwise she looks fine. Happy, even. As if nothing had happened.

As if being naked in front of two teenage boys isn't worth a second thought. He hopes that isn't true.

"No, for what happened at the lake," he says.

"Not your fault," Chloe says. "And I handled it."

"I should have—" Sid starts.

"Should have what? Defended my honor?" Chloe makes air quotes around the words. Sid nods.

"Something like that," he mumbles.

Chloe grins and sticks her tongue out at him. "What makes you think I've got any honor left to defend?"

Sid blushes and says, "I'm sorry" again as Chloe hops on her bike and rides off toward her house.

He walks his bike down the driveway, trying to put off the moment when he will have to confront Wain. When he gets to the house, he sees Megan's bike on its side in the rose bed beside the front steps. A single pink rose lies in the dirt next to the handlebars, broken off by the bicycle's fall. Megan doesn't look kindly on damage to her flowers—so few survive the local deer. Sid puts both bikes away, brushes the dirt off the rose and goes inside to put it in some water.

The house is quiet. A note on the table says, *Gone to the store with F for ice cream. Pls pick some rasps for short-cake and some toms. XO M. PS What happened at the lake?*

Sid crumples up the note, throws it in the garbage and goes to take a shower. The door to Wain's room is shut. Wain can stay in his room for the rest of his visit, as far as Sid is concerned.

When Megan and Fariza get back from the store, Sid is in the garden, picking raspberries. Fariza joins him, solemnly peering into the lower branches and plucking berries that have escaped Sid's gaze. Soon they have more than enough for the shortcake.

"Did you have fun today, Fariza?" he asks as they turn to go back to the house.

Fariza nods and points at him. Her fingernails are the soft pink of the tiny shells he used to collect on the beach when he was small. Chloe must have painted them.

"Me? Not so much," he says. "Chloe and Wain had a fight."

Fariza frowns. The tiny furrow between her eyebrows looks like two small exclamation points. He reaches out to rub it away and Fariza pulls back slightly. It's her first instinct—to pull away from contact—and Sid still has no idea why.

Her mouth opens and closes a few times before she takes a deep breath and says, "Fighting is bad."

It takes all Sid's willpower not to pick her up and hug her, but he knows it's too soon. Instead, he says, "You're right. Fighting is bad. But sometimes people fight. It'll be okay."

Fariza clenches her small hands into fists. "It's not okay."

Sid waits for her to say more, and when she doesn't, he starts walking back to the house. He has only taken a few steps when Fariza comes up beside him and places her hand in his. "Don't tell anyone," she says.

"Not even Megan?" he asks.

"Not even Megan," she says as they climb the back stairs.

Why all the secrets? Sid wonders as he slices ripe toma-toes and washes lettuce from the garden. First Chloe and now Fariza. Is it a girl thing? He can understand—sort of—why Chloe doesn't want anyone to know about what happened at the lake. But Fariza? Why would she want to hide the fact that she's talking again? He sighs and checks the barbecue. Almost ready. Caleb comes outside with a plate of burger patties. Megan sets down a tray of drinks—lemonade, iced tea, water, beer—and plastic glasses. Fariza follows with a basket of buns. Elizabeth carries out a steaming bowl of corn-on-the cob, while Wain lurks in a corner of the porch, listening to his iPod.

"Chloe not joining us?" Caleb asks when the burgers are done and everyone is seated.

"I don't think so," Sid says. "She's obsessing about her hair."

"What's wrong with her hair?"

"Beats me," Sid says. "You know what girls are like."

"That I do," Caleb says. "My sister Jo used to iron her hair and then check for split ends with a magnifying glass. And now look at her."

Sid laughs. His Aunt Jo had moved to Hawaii years ago to run scuba charters. She's the least feminine woman he's ever seen. Also the strongest. Megan turns and looks at him, one eyebrow raised, her lips pursed. He knows that look. The look says, *You can't fool me. I know something is wrong, and I wish you'd talk to me, but I'm not going to pry.* He meets her gaze and shrugs slightly. He feels a bit bloated, as if the secrets he is carrying are expanding in his gut. Or maybe he's just hungry.

Dinner is awkward. Wain's manners haven't improved and Elizabeth is obviously embarrassed.

"Elbows, dear," she murmurs. And, "You have a napkin."

Wain ignores her, bolting his burger and getting up from the table before anyone else has finished, leaving his dirty dishes behind. He refuses to even look at Sid. Fariza, who is clearly puzzled by the ear of corn on her plate, glances up at Wain as he leaves the table and goes inside. She taps Sid's arm and points at Wain's plate, where a crumpled napkin sits in a blob of ketchup. She frowns, and shakes her finger at the dirty dishes, as if they are naughty children. Her corn remains untouched. It occurs to Sid that maybe she has never eaten corn on the cob before.

"So, Fariza," Sid says, "there are two ways to eat corn. The right way—across the cob—and the wrong way—around the cob. Allow me to demonstrate."

He slathers an ear of corn with butter, sprinkles it with salt and pepper and starts to eat, going from one side to the other, the cob moving like the carriage of an old typewriter. "Ding!" he says when he reaches the end of a row. "Now you try."

Fariza dutifully butters and seasons her cob and sinks her teeth into the soft, sweet kernels. Her eyes widen as she chews, and before long she has made a narrow path across the cob. Butter drips off her hands and down her chin.

"Ding!" Fariza says when she reaches the end of her second row. Everyone stops eating to stare at her. She grins and declares, "Corn is good." A kernel is stuck to her upper lip and the tip of her nose is shiny with butter.

Elizabeth clasps her hands together, Caleb drops his cob of corn on the floor and Sid does what he didn't do in the raspberry patch earlier: he grabs Fariza around the waist and waltzes her around the table.

Megan pulls Caleb and Elizabeth to their feet, where they form a circle around Sid and Fariza, chanting, "Corn is good! Corn is good!" Fariza giggles as they all aim kisses at her greasy cheeks. "That's the most beautiful sentence I've ever heard," Megan says when they finally stop whirling, and Sid plops Fariza back in her place at the table. "This calls for a celebration. Sid, could you give me a hand?"

Sid follows Megan into the kitchen, where she gives him a rib-crushing hug before setting him to work whipping the cream. "You knew, didn't you?" she asks as she rummages in the junk drawer for some candles. "You knew she could speak."

"Yeah," Sid says. "She talked a bit when we were picking raspberries, but she swore me to secrecy. I'm sorry. I wanted to tell you, but, you know…I couldn't." And I can't tell you about Wain and Chloe either, he thinks.

He can't imagine that either of them is going to talk about what happened at the lake anytime soon. He's not sure he wants them to anyway. Maybe Chloe's right. Maybe it's no big deal.

"She trusted you," Megan says. "And it made her feel safe. Safe enough to talk to us. You were right not to say anything."

"And who knows," Sid says. "Maybe 'Corn is good' is all she has to say."

Sid turns the speed up on the mixer, but he can still hear Megan say, "It's a start anyway. Now, how many candles should I put on the shortcake?"

"So. The dummy can talk now?" Wain is sitting at the kitchen table the next morning, shoveling cornflakes into his mouth. He and Sid are alone. Fariza and Elizabeth are still asleep and Megan and Caleb have taken their coffee onto the porch.

"Don't be an asshole," Sid says wearily. He puts some bread in the toaster and gets out the peanut butter and honey.

"You fighting with your girlfriend?" Wain asks. He wipes his mouth with the back of his hand and belches loudly.

"She's not my girlfriend."

"Oh, that's right. Girl like that needs a man, not some faggy artist. What's with all your notebooks anyway, you and what's-her-name?"

The toast pops up and Sid jumps at the sound. Wain laughs. It's a nasty noise, jagged as a broken bone.

"Her name's Fariza." Sid picks up the toast, burning his fingers.

"I know," Wain says agreeably. "You guys drawing today?"

"Probably."

Wain pushes himself back from the table and saunters out of the room. "I might join you," he says as he goes. "Devi taught me some stuff."

Sid takes a bite of his toast and wills Fariza to sleep till noon. Perhaps by then Wain will have lost interest or Caleb will have taken him out on the boat. What Sid really wants to do, after he's finished illustrating the stories in Fariza's notebook, is start a fresh notebook of his own. He wants to draw what he sees around him, not what goes on inside his head. There must be a way of doing both, but he hasn't figured it out yet. He has completely lost interest in Billy, who is doomed to stay in Titan Arum with the giant smelly plant and the horrible people. He must have finished at least ten Billy books over the years. It might be time to burn them or shred them, although that seems a cruel end for his companion of so many years.

He finishes his toast and puts his dishes (and Wain's) in the dishwasher. He's sorting laundry when Fariza appears, one hand clutching Fred, the other holding her notebook.

"Can we draw?" she says. Her voice is a bit raspy, but no more so than Sid's when he first speaks in the morning.

"Sure," Sid says. "Breakfast first though, okay?"

"Okay." Fariza trots off to the kitchen where he can hear her ask Megan for some cereal. He wonders how long it will be before they all forget that she once had a vocabulary of only three words.

There are two more *Fred and Fariza* stories in Fariza's notebook: *Fred and Fariza Go Fishing* and *Fred and Fariza at the Spa*. When he draws Chloe applying a seaweed wrap to Fred's skinny legs, he remembers the last thing Chloe said to him, and his face burns. He finishes a sketch of Fariza painting Chloe's toenails, and then he starts to close the book.

"There's more," Fariza says.

He turns the page. It's blank. "No, there isn't."

She takes the notebook from him, turns it over and opens it from the back. Her wobbly printing covers the first page.

"Read it," she says.

I was coffing one day. I had a sore throte. I got sent home from school. Mami tucked me into bed and brot me a glass of juice. The red kind I like. She and my sister Parveen were talking in the living room. I think Mami was crying, but it could have been Parveen. She stays out late. Papi and Amir—my brother—yell at her a lot and call her bad names. Mami gets upset, but she never calls Parveen bad names. I heard the front door slam. Everybody was screaming: Mami, Papi, Amir and Parveen. I pulled the cuvvers over my head. There were two big booms. Then the front door slammed again.

Sid stops reading at the end of the first page. A bitter taste fills his mouth—as if his saliva has curdled. He can't read any more. He doesn't want to know what happens next. He's a coward.

Make It Stop

Fariza's hand quivers as she turns the page. Her small voice fills the quiet room.

"I stayed in my room under the covers a long time. Then I had to pee really bad. So I got up and opened my door. Mami and Parveen were lying on the living-room floor. I tried to wake them up but I couldn't. I started to scream. Mrs. Marshall, from next door, came and pulled me away from Mami and Parveen. I heard the sirens. Mrs. Marshall took me to her apartment and made me hot tea with a lot of sugar. The police came and talked to me. I told them about Papi and Amir yelling at Parveen and Mami. I told them about the two big booms.

"I slept on Mrs. Marshall's blue couch. In the morning, a woman came and told me that Mami and Parveen were dead. I wanted Papi, but she said he and Amir were in jail.

I wanted to stay with Mrs. Marshall, but I couldn't. She has two jobs and three little kids already. So I went to stay with strangers. I always said please and thank you. I wanted Mami and Papi to be proud of me." Fariza's voice wavers as she closes the book.

Sid doesn't know what to do or say. Vomit rises in his throat, but he chokes it back. Fariza is sitting very still, her hands resting on the notebook.

"Do you hate me now?" she asks when Sid doesn't speak.

"Hate you?"

"Because of what I did." Fariza starts to cry. She rocks back and forth, making a noise like a hurt kitten. Sid wants to wrap his arms around her, but he is afraid it might frighten her. She crawls into his lap and buries her face in his chest as he grasps for words. He understands now why she has chosen not to speak. Words are so inadequate, so insubstantial in the face of such pain. Words can't protect you. They can't clean your wounds or quench your thirst. They can't stroke your hair or wipe the tears from your face. Words fly out of your mouth and evaporate. And still he has to try.

"No, no, no, no," he manages to say. "You didn't do anything wrong."

"But I didn't get out of bed," she wails. "I didn't help Mami and Parveen. And I told the police about Papi and Amir."

"You were right to stay in your room," Sid says. "I don't think you could have helped Mami and Parveen.

And it wasn't wrong to tell the police about your dad and brother. Not if they hurt your mother and sister." There are so many things he wants to say: *Your father and brother are evil; they would have killed you too; you're better off here.* Maybe someday he'll be able to say those things to her, but for now he searches for something simple, something innocent that will comfort her.

All he can think of is a song Megan used to sing to him when he was cranky or upset, a song that always calmed him down. He still remembers all the words.

> *When you're down and troubled*
> *And you need a helping hand*
> *And nothing, nothing is going right.*

When he gets to the part about people trying to take your soul, he wishes he hadn't started, but he keeps singing until the end.

> *Ain't it good to know you've got a friend.*
> *You've got a friend.*

By the time he stops singing, Fariza is asleep in his arms. He is about to stand up and carry her to her room, when he hears someone clapping.

"Trust you to know all the words to that dumb hippie song. What are you—sixty?" Wain says.

Sid brushes past him, taking care not to bump Fariza against the door frame. "Shut up, Wain," he says. He climbs the stairs and tucks Fariza into her bed, nestling Fred next to her under the duvet. When he goes back downstairs, Wain has disappeared. Megan is in the kitchen, wiping the counters.

"Caleb says he can take you and Wain out on the *Caprice* today. Elizabeth and Fariza and I are having lunch with Irena and Chloe. Where is Fariza anyway?"

"She was tired, so I put her back to bed. You know how crabby she can be if she doesn't get enough sleep."

Megan nods. "You look as if you could use a bit more shut-eye yourself, buddy. Everything okay?"

The weight of Fariza's story is suffocating him, but all he says is, "Yeah, I didn't sleep very well last night. I don't feel much like going out on the boat. Will Caleb mind?"

"You know how rare it is for Caleb to get a day off this time of year," she says. "He really wants to do this. He thinks it might help."

"Help what?"

"Help you and Wain figure out your relationship."

"I already figured it out. We share some DNA. That's it."

"You know there's more to it than that," she says.

"Not if I don't want there to be. He's a jerk."

"Yes, he is," Megan says. "But not all the time." She folds the dishrag and hangs it from the faucet. "So do this for Elizabeth."

"For Elizabeth?"

"She thinks you're good for Wain."

"You're kidding, right? Wain thinks I'm a loser. No, wait, he's upgraded me to a loser hippie. And I think he's a psycho. I can't wait for him to leave."

"And Elizabeth?"

"I'll visit her. She can come back here."

"Her life is in Victoria, Sid. Yours is here. Wain is the bridge. Think about it."

"Yeah, a bridge I'd like to jump off."

"Sid." Megan's voice has a note of rebuke in it.

"Okay, okay," he says. "But I'm going for a bike ride first. Tell Caleb I'll be back in an hour."

Caleb honks the horn, and Sid lugs a cooler down the front steps to the van. No way is Wain riding shotgun this time. The front seat is covered in an old beach towel and the backseat is buried under a crab trap. The van smells as if someone has set up a brewery in a fish-packing plant. Orange float vests are piled on top of coolers filled with empty bottles. Tangled ropes snake around yellow deck boots stuffed with rolled-up charts.

It's always like this when Caleb gets back from a charter. He just throws everything in the back of the van and sorts it out after he takes the clients to the pub for one last beer.

Sid heaves the cooler into the back, moving aside a pail with a dead fish in it.

"Can I chuck this?" he says, holding up the pail.

Caleb turns around, peers into the bucket and grimaces. "Forgot about that one. Let's dump it at the wharf."

Sid climbs into the front seat and slams the door as Wain comes down the front stairs. He glares at Sid and yanks the crab trap off the backseat.

"It reeks in here," he says.

"Welcome to my world," Caleb says with a smile.

When they get to the boat, Caleb hands them both orange flotation vests. Sid puts his on without argument. He knows the rules.

"Life jackets are for pussies," Wain says.

Caleb slips his arms into a vest. "So I must be a pussy," he says. "Better a pussy in a life jacket than a drowned pussy, I always say. You want to go or not?"

Wain zips up his vest as Sid and Caleb prepare to leave the dock.

"Spent much time around boats, Wain?" Caleb asks.

"A bit," Wain says.

"Rowboats," Sid mutters.

"First and only rule is this," Caleb continues. "The captain is always right."

Wain snickers and salutes. Caleb raises an eyebrow at him. "Cast off then, sailor. Let's get this party started."

They pull away from the wharf, heading for the strait. As they pass the islet in the mouth of the cove, Sid says, "I'm gonna catch some zees. Wake me up for lunch."

Caleb nods. "We're going to head up to the Narrows, take a look at Ripple Rock—Elizabeth wants some pictures, even though there's nothing much to see—and then duck in behind Maud Island."

"Sounds good," Sid says. He climbs down into the galley and makes his way to the bow of the boat. He opens a door with a small hand-painted sign: *Sid's Space*. The triangular stateroom is both tiny and tidy. He reaches into a small hammock that serves as a bedside table, extracts a piece of Juicy Fruit gum and lies down on the bunk, snapping his gum and listening to the growl of the engine and the slap of water against the hull of the boat. He often falls asleep when he is out on the *Caprice*, and after a nap on board he always feels rejuvenated, as if under the influence of a powerful yet beneficial drug.

When he closes his eyes, he dreams that he and Devi are snorkeling inside a reef in some tropical paradise. The water is warm and clear and full of fish that seem to have no fear of the strange, clumsy creatures in goggles and fins. A huge school of fish shaped like enormous darning needles surrounds him, and for a moment he panics, afraid that he will be pierced and that his blood will draw the sharks that lurk beyond the reef. He uses his rubber fins to propel himself toward the beach, and when he looks back, Devi is gone. He swims back out to where the needle fish had swarmed and finds nothing—no sign that Devi had been there five minutes ago, swimming with the clown fish and laughing at Sid's cowardice. Sid screams Devi's name, but there is no reply. He rips off his snorkel and

mask and dives into the silence of the reef, scattering a
school of tiny yellow fish and disturbing a small octopus
whose tentacles brush his arm as he swims by. A green
sea turtle swims toward him, impossibly graceful in its
huge shell. It nudges him with its extraterrestrial head
and speaks to him. "Wake up," it says. "We're here."
For once, Sid is glad to hear Wain's voice.

They are anchored behind Maud Island; Caleb has
put up the cockpit table and opened the cooler. "Help
yourselves, boys," he says, grabbing a sandwich and a
Coke. "We'll row to shore after lunch. See what's what."

Sid takes a bite of a turkey sandwich. A single gull
circles the boat, waiting for scraps.

"Sid, you should tell Wain how the *Caprice* got her
name."

Sid knows Caleb is trying to make him interact with
Wain. He doesn't want to, but he also doesn't want to
upset Caleb.

"Aye aye, Captain," Sid says. "So, Megan is obsessed
with this book called *The Curve of Time*. It's about some
woman who took all her kids—she had, like, six of them,
I think, and a dog—up and down the coast in her boat.
It was called the *Caprice*. She was always sending her kids
off in the dinghy to play on some remote beach while she
cooked dinner or repaired the engine."

Caleb takes up the story. "No life jackets, ever.
Drinking from streams. Running away from bears.
Climbing moss-covered cliffs looking for huckleberries.

Shooting some of the most dangerous rapids on the coast. It's a wonder they survived. They even took artifacts from Indian villages. It was years ago—a different time—but it still makes me cringe to think about those kids crawling around in abandoned burial boxes.

"A few years ago, Megan decided it would be fun to recreate some of the original *Caprice*'s voyages. You know, take a bunch of local kids, spend the summer on the water. Sort of like a mini Outward Bound. This was before I had the charter business, when I was still working in town. She studied the charts until she knew them inside out and backward and she practically memorized the whole book. Remember that time she took you, Sid?"

Sid takes a bite of a cookie. Peanut-butter chocolate-chip. His favorite. "Yeah, I remember. It was a nightmare," he says. "I hid in my bunk most of the time, hoping that a big storm would wash the other three kids overboard. I was only ten. They were a lot older and they thought I was a freak. They liked to piss on the skylight over my bunk. Especially if it was open. Their idea of a good time was lighting up a joint when they thought Megan wasn't looking and throwing pop cans at seagulls."

"Yeah, but Sid got his revenge," Caleb says, tapping the back of Sid's wrist with his can of Coke. "Megan was pretty angry at him," he says, turning to Wain, "but those kids were jerks."

"So what did you do?" Wain asks. He has been unusually quiet since they anchored, and he's only picked at his food. Sid wonders if he is seasick. He hopes so.

"I hijacked the *Caprice*," Sid says simply. "We were anchored in Teakerne Arm and Megan sent the guys to shore in the dinghy one afternoon—told them how to find the little lake. I could tell she was pretty sick of them too. They didn't like her cooking, they complained about sleeping in bunks, they hated not having TV and Internet access. As soon as she saw they were safely landed, she went to have a nap. I watched them leave the beach and then I slipped over the railing and swam to shore. I was a good swimmer, even then. I rowed the dinghy back to the boat, pulled up the anchor, started the engine and chugged away, all without waking Megan up.

"I had to stand on a crab trap to see over the wheel. After about an hour Megan woke up. You should have seen the look on her face!" Sid opens his eyes very wide and makes a perfect O with his mouth. "Man, she was pissed! She grabbed the wheel, turned us around and opened up the throttle. It was dark when we got back to the beach and those guys were freaking out. I mean really freaking out. Sobbing, calling for their mommies, bargaining with God. Megan made me row in to get them. I had to promise to tell them what I'd done. I thought they'd kill me, but they were so glad to be rescued they didn't do a thing. Never even threw a pop can at my head. We went home the next morning, and they never told anyone what happened. I guess they were afraid I'd tell someone what pussies they were. Gave them a whole new respect for freaks."

"No kidding," Wain says, just before he leans over the side of the boat and pukes.

By All Means

Wain spends the rest of the trip lying in one of the bunks, puking into a bucket.

"Not much of a sailor, is he?" Caleb remarks.

"Not much opportunity, I guess," Sid says. "Other than rowboats and BC Ferries." He's feeling a little sorry for Wain, whose moans are pathetic. "Almost there," he yells over the engine noise.

When they get to the wharf, he helps Caleb get the *Caprice* safely docked before he goes below to rescue Wain, who is sitting up, his head in his hands.

"Ready to go?" Sid says.

Wain nods and stands up, grabbing Sid's arm to keep from falling.

"This sucks," he says as he climbs up the stairs and flops like a dead fish into the cockpit.

Sid tries not to laugh as Wain crawls over to a stanchion and pulls himself onto the deck, where he peers down at the space between the boat and the wharf. The water glistens with oil. The fumes from a nearby outboard motor make him gag.

Sid jumps off the boat and Wain yelps. "Don't do that!"

"Do what?" Sid asks.

"Make the boat rock."

Sid laughs. "You coming?"

"In a minute," Wain says. He vomits into the oily water, straightens up and extends his hand to Sid, who helps him off the boat without comment. It's the first time Wain has touched him without intent to cause pain. As soon as he is safely on shore, Wain climbs into the back of the van and curls himself into a ball. Sid empties the fish bucket and places it next to Wain. When they get to the house, Wain runs, doubled over, up the stairs and into the bathroom.

Megan comes out of the War Room and shuts the door behind her. "Fariza's asleep on the couch. She had a rough day. What's wrong with Wain?"

"Turns out Wain gets seasick," Sid says. "What's up with Fariza?"

"She wanted to show me something after you left, but she wouldn't say what it was. She just kept saying *It's gone. It's gone.* But I couldn't help her find it, because I didn't know what I was looking for and she wouldn't tell me.

She's been sitting at the window, crying, all afternoon, waiting for you to come back. I finally got her to lie down and she went to sleep. Did you have fun?"

"Yeah. It was okay except for Wain getting seasick. I told him about ditching those guys at Teakerne Arm. And lunch was good."

"Thanks, Sid," Megan says. "When Fariza wakes up, maybe you can help her solve the mystery of the missing—whatever it is."

"Sure," Sid says, although it's no mystery to him. Fariza must be looking for her notebook, which she left on the dining-room table after she read it to Sid.

The field of suspects is small. Very small.

Dinner is a quiet meal. Elizabeth is at Irena's. For all her talk of wanting to relax, Elizabeth clearly prefers to be busy. In Irena she has found, if not a soul mate, then at least a playmate. Today they made jam; tonight they are going to have dinner with a pack of Irena's cronies, who call themselves the Pink Panthers. No one is quite sure why. Elizabeth has been made an honorary member. Sid wonders if Chloe helped make the jam or if she was out with her friends all day. Maybe they're catching a movie in town tonight or making a bonfire on the beach, roasting marshmallows, drinking beer. He doesn't like hanging out with her friends, but he still wishes he was with her rather than sitting with Megan and Caleb and a silent Fariza. Wain is still going back and forth from his room to the bathroom. Sid will have to wait to ask him what he did with Fariza's notebook.

The next morning when Sid gets up, Elizabeth is sitting in the War Room, talking on the phone. She is hunched over, with her back to the door. Her voice is low, but Sid can make out some of the words. *Hospital. Wain. Medication.* It doesn't take a genius to figure it out: Devi is back.

Megan confirms his suspicions. "She wants to leave right after breakfast. Wain doesn't know yet. I suggested that they stay a day or two longer, give Devi a chance to stabilize, but she's adamant. I can understand that—Devi's her daughter—but Wain needs time to adjust. I told her she could leave him here for a while. Maybe until school starts."

"Leave him here? Why? Devi's his mom. He should be with her."

"And she can't look after him right now. That's pretty clear. We've got room. And time."

Sid opens his mouth to object, but Megan cuts him off. "That's what we do, Sid. You know that."

"But this is different," he says. "You know it is."

"Different how? Because he's your brother? I get that. I do. But it's all the more reason to help him. Your grandmother can't look after him—she needs to be with Devi. And Phil clearly isn't prepared to take Wain on, and I can't say I blame him. Would you rather Wain went home and got into real trouble?"

Sid shakes his head. He knows he's not going to win this argument. The best he can hope for is that Wain will refuse to stay.

Elizabeth comes out of the War Room, her hair loose around her shoulders. She appears to have shrunk, or maybe it's an illusion created by the fact that she is wearing one of Caleb's old fleece jackets over her long white nightgown. She manages a weak smile. "Excuse my ensemble. I came down to answer the phone and I got so cold I grabbed the first thing I could find. And I have a terrible headache. I should have known better than to stay out so late with those old girls," she says. "The Gray Matter Granny couldn't begin to keep up."

"Stay another day at least," Megan says. "Devi's in the hospital, right?"

Elizabeth nods. "Phil says she was at the house when he came back from Vancouver. She was in her studio, smashing her work with a hammer. He says she's skin and bones, and very depressed. He took her to the hospital and she was admitted to the psych ward. She's been there before. They've started the lithium." Tears trickle down her cheeks. "My sweet girl. She hates lithium, but it's the only thing that works."

Megan puts her arm around the older woman and leads her into the kitchen.

Sid follows them and starts making toast for everybody.

"Should I call Wain?" he asks when he's buttered the last slice and put the toast on the table with a jar of peanut butter and a dish of the jam Irena and Elizabeth made the day before. "And Fariza?"

"Let them sleep," Megan says. "They need it. Fariza is upset about losing something," she explains to Elizabeth. "Some days are better than others. I was so encouraged when she started to talk, but she still has a long way to go."

"I know what she's lost," Sid says, "and I'm pretty sure where to find it." He doesn't want to accuse Wain— he just wants to get the notebook back before Wain leaves. Then things can return to normal. Even as he thinks it, he knows it's not possible. The minute Phil arrived on their doorstep, normal took a hike. Headed for the hills. Said, "*Hasta la vista, baby. Sayonara.*" A picture forms in Sid's mind of Billy, poor sad Billy, trudging up the side of a mountain. The caption says *Farewell to Normaltown.* Goodbye, Billy. Hello, Sid.

"I'm not going." Wain is sitting at the kitchen table in a T-shirt and boxers, a piece of jam-laden toast halfway to his mouth. "You can't make me."

Sid watches the other adults at the table consider Wain's statement. Wain is big for his age, and strong. No doubt Caleb could force him into Elizabeth's car, but Caleb has already left with another charter. The idea of

Megan and Elizabeth wrangling Wain into the car makes Sid giggle. Could they even pick him up? He doubts it.

"What's so funny, man?" Wain growls.

"Nothing," Sid says, but the image is playing in his head like a scene from a lame horror movie: Elizabeth dragging Wain by the arms, Megan clutching his feet, Wain twisting in their grip, gnashing his teeth and screaming. *The Mommies' Revenge.* He laughs out loud and Megan frowns at him. It's clearly not a good morning for humor.

Sid puts his dishes in the dishwasher. "You need me for anything?" he asks Megan. When she shakes her head, he says, "I'm going for a bike ride. Might stop in and see Chloe. What ferry you guys gonna catch?"

"Didn't you hear me?" Wain says. "I'm not going."

"Perhaps the three o'clock?" Elizabeth says. "I'm not sure. I want to say goodbye to Irena. You've all been so kind." She reaches out and touches Sid's hand. "You'll be back before we leave, won't you?"

He nods. "For sure."

"Good." She stands and clears her dishes. "I'll just have a bath in that lovely tub of yours before I get organized then. It's such a lovely view—all that sky and ocean. Wain, dear, why don't you have a shower?"

"I don't need one," Wain says. "Are you deaf, Nana? I'm not going. I want to stay here." His voice is losing its bluster. He's pleading now, like a kid who wants to stay up past his bedtime.

"I wish we could," Elizabeth says. "I truly do. But your mother needs us."

"Needs you, maybe," Wain says, pushing away from the table. His chair falls backward and he kicks it out of the way as he runs from the room.

Elizabeth puts her head in her hands. "I'm not sure I can do this," she says softly.

"Then don't," Megan says. "Wain can stay here. I'll drive him down myself in time for school. Believe me, I'm used to this kind of thing. You should have seen Sid when he was Wain's age." She rolls her eyes. "Talk about mood swings! He put any teenage girl to shame."

Sid is astonished. "I was never like that," he protests, although even as he speaks he knows she is right. He used to go days without speaking, and then he'd get into a fight with Megan or Caleb or one of the other kids in the house. The fights were always about something stupid, like whether he needed a haircut or how often he washed his clothes or why an older kid got to stay up and watch a movie.

"What helped?" Elizabeth asks.

"Not sure," Megan says. "Sid can probably answer that better than I can. Sid?"

Sid thinks for a minute before he answers. "Drawing helped. A lot. Riding my bike. Hanging out with Chloe. Helping Caleb on the boat. Now I just try not to take my bad moods out on anyone else. Wain's not there yet."

And he may never get there, Sid thinks. It would be cruel to say it.

"Give him some time," Megan says.

Sid rides up to the lake but doesn't swim. It's one of Megan and Caleb's hard and fast rules: No swimming solo. Not that they would ever know, but he doesn't feel like getting wet. Or betraying their trust. He just wants to sit by himself and listen to the water lap the shore, sift the beach stones through his fingers, watch the dragonflies skim the surface of the lake. He sits for an hour, the sun on his face. I should have put on some sunscreen, he thinks. Or worn a hat. He'll burn if he stays out much longer, so he rides back toward his house, wondering if he should stop and see Chloe. Tell her that Wain and Elizabeth are leaving.

He stops at the end of the long driveway leading to her house. He's spent half his childhood there. Why is he so hesitant to do what he's done a thousand times before: ride up to the front door, open it and call out, "Anybody home?" No matter who is there—Chloe, Irena or Esther—someone will always reply, "In here, Sid," and he will be offered a cold drink on a hot day or vice versa. Esther might be playing old show tunes on her saxophone in the dining room or she might be curled up on the window seat with a book and a glass of wine. Irena might call him into the kitchen to help prepare and eat whatever meal is in the works. Chloe might drag him up to her room and ask for his opinion on a new hairstyle or an actor in a TV show he hasn't seen. No doubt she'll complain about her family, which Sid finds mystifying.

Today he lifts his hand off the brass doorknob, knocks twice and waits for someone to answer.

"What's wrong with you?" Chloe opens the door and frowns at him. "Since when do you knock? I was doing my nails and now they're all smudged." She holds up her right hand—the polish is smeared. "I'm going to have to start all over."

"Sorry," Sid says. "You going Goth on me?" Chloe calls herself Pretty in Pink or Pink Lady, movie references that had to be explained to Sid. Black nail polish is something she might wear on Halloween, but not in the middle of August.

"Maybe." Chloe grins. "I'm thinking of going the whole Dita Von Teese route. You know: black hair, lots of eye makeup, dark red lipstick. Craig thinks she's hot."

"If I knew who Dita Von what's-her-name was, I could comment," Sid says. "But I wish you wouldn't. Dye your hair black, I mean. Your hair is beautiful." And Craig's a douche, he wants to add.

Chloe blushes and touches her hair. "You think?"

"Yeah, but I also think you just got nail polish in it."

"Crap." Chloe slams the door and marches up to her room. "You coming?" she calls back to Sid. "You can do my toes."

Can't Make Me

"You can work at our spa if you like," Chloe says. She's sitting on her bed, her feet on a blue towel. Sid is bent over Chloe's feet, concentrating on applying a clear top coat to her nails. She is right about one thing: he is good at pedicures. He has a steady hand, even though touching her foot is making him sweat. But there's no way he's working in her spa. He can just imagine what Wain would say.

"I'm serious, Sid. Mom says I can set up a day spa on the porch—for teens only. I'm going to call it Spaaaah! You know, like it's super relaxing. Fariza's going to be my helper. We're going to offer all-natural facials—chocolate or lemon—a cranberry body scrub—arms and legs only—manicures and pedicures. Irena said we couldn't do the seaweed wrap or the hot-stone thing. Something about lawsuits."

"How did you learn how to do all this stuff?"

"YouTube," Chloe says. "And an article in an old *Oprah* magazine. It's not like it's rocket science."

"Or brain surgery," Sid says. It's an old joke of theirs, the rocket-science-brain-surgery thing, something they've been saying since they were little kids. He sits back and screws the cap back on the polish. "You're done."

Chloe looks down at her feet. The polish isn't actually black—it's a deep, dark blue called Russian Navy. "Awesome job," she says. "Very glam. So—you in?"

Sid shakes his head. "Nah. I wouldn't be any good at the chitchat."

Chloe wiggles her toes at him and grins. "You're probably right. Maybe you could do a poster for us? Or some flyers? I'm gonna put them on the ferry and at the store."

"That I can do," Sid says. "As soon as Wain leaves."

"He's leaving? When?"

"Today. Devi came back. She's in the hospital. Elizabeth wants to go right away—on the three o'clock ferry. Wain says he won't go. Megan told him he could stay. I left before they worked it all out."

"Wow. If my mom was sick, I'd want to be with her."

"Yeah, but your mom's not crazy," Sid says. "Not even close."

"You don't have to live with her," Chloe says. "And Devi's your mom too. Did you forget that?"

Sid stares at her. "Whose side are you on? Devi's not my mom."

Chloe removes the cotton balls from between her toes and slips her flip-flops on her feet. "You and Wain are acting like five-year-olds." She pretends to cry, screwing her fists into her eyes. "*Wah! Wah! Wah! I don't have a perfect family. I'm going to run away.*"

"It's not like that," Sid says. "I'm not running away from anything." The minute he says it, he realizes it's a lie.

"So what are you going to do? Hide out here all day? Let's go." She grabs Sid's arm and propels him out the door and down the stairs. "Get my bike. I gotta leave a note for Mom."

"You are so bossy," Sid says.

"That's what you love about me," Chloe replies. "Now get going."

It's true, he thinks as he gets her bike from the garage, I do love that about her. That and a lot of other things. She always knows what to do and say: Let's make a fort, Sid. Let's go to the lake. Don't step in the dog shit. Keep your fingers out of the cookie dough. Do my nails. Get me my bike. He wonders if it's a bad thing that he likes being ordered around.

Chloe comes out of the house and jumps on her bike. "Let's go, dude," she says. "Time's a wastin'."

He follows her down the long driveway. The poplar trees rustle in the breeze. The air smells faintly of the seaweed fertilizer Irena puts on her raspberry bushes. He wishes he could stop and pick some berries, but Chloe is racing ahead, standing up to pedal.

When they get to his house, Elizabeth meets them on the porch.

"I was just about to call your house, Chloe. Wain's disappeared. Megan has taken my car to go and look for him. I'm here with Fariza and she's very upset. She keeps asking for you, Sid. Can you stay with her while I go and look for Wain?"

"I'll stay, Mrs. Eikenboom," Chloe says. "You and Sid go and look for Wain. She'll be fine."

"Are you sure, dear?" Elizabeth says.

"Positive," Chloe says. She leaves Sid on the porch with his grandmother. They can hear her call out, "Fariza, sweetie, let's make popsicles. Then you can braid my hair."

"How long has he been gone?" Sid asks.

Elizabeth shakes her head. "We're not sure. I was in the bath for a while, and then I had a cup of coffee with Megan. I thought Wain was upstairs packing, but when I went to look for him, he was gone. Megan left about an hour ago to look for him. He didn't take the bike, so he can't have gone too far. Can he?" She sits down heavily on one of the porch chairs. "What if he tried hitchhiking? Oh, Sid, I'm too old for this."

Sid squats down beside her. Today she looks old and sort of deflated—not like the Gray Matter Granny at all. She has pulled her hair back into a scraggly ponytail. The wrinkles on her cheeks seem deeper than when he first met her. Her eyes are hooded and tired.

"You stay here," Sid says. "I think I might know where he's gone, and it's easier for me to go alone. And when I find him, I'm going to drag him back here and stuff him into the car for you. Okay?" He goes to the kitchen to fill his water bottle and grab a nectarine. "Chloe," he calls, "I'm going to look for Wain. Elizabeth's still here. Is Fariza okay?"

Chloe's voice floats down the stairs. "She's okay. I'm reading her a story. Good luck."

Sid jumps on his bike and heads to the wharf, where he borrows a rowboat from one of the fishermen. In ten minutes he is dragging the rowboat onto the islet's rocky beach, where a blue kayak is tied to a low arbutus branch.

"Wain," he yells. "I know you're here. This is getting old."

He stomps up the beach and follows a path around the islet, which is much smaller than Jimmy Chicken. It's so small it doesn't even have a name. He smells smoke before he sees the fire.

"What the fuck, Wain!" He speeds up, almost tripping on a root in the path. In a clearing on the far side of the island, Wain is hunched over a small fire, feeding it with twigs.

"Are you insane?" Sid yells. "It's August! You can't have a fire!"

Wain turns and says, "Oh, hey, it's Smokey the Bear," as he adds a twig to the fire. "Sorry about that, Smokey. Didn't think you'd mind. I mean, this island is kind of a dump."

Sid looks around for something to carry water in—there's nothing but a battered yogurt container. He scoops up some water and empties it onto the fire, which is actually pretty small. Wain isn't much of a boy scout. Sid runs back and forth to the ocean, filling and emptying the container until the fire is out. Wain does nothing to stop him—or to help—until Sid orders him to smother the fire with sand and stones. When he is sure the fire is out, he sits down on a rock and says, "You're a useless piece of shit, you know."

Wain says nothing.

"You took Fariza's book, didn't you?"

Wain nods and sits down beside Sid on the rock. Sid moves away. He's so angry that he has to clench his hands together to keep from punching Wain. Even from a few feet away, he can feel the heat of Wain's body, smell his sweat. "You stink," he says. "Where's the book?"

"At the house. Under my bed. Except for this." He reaches into the back pocket of his jeans, pulls out some crumpled pages and hands them to Sid. "I heard you reading her story. I picked up the book after you took her upstairs. I couldn't stop thinking about it. How scared she must have been. Must still be. I mean, her mother's dead. Her sister's dead. Her father and brother killed them. I thought it would help to burn the words, like, burn away the pain. Devi did that once—burned some letters she got from my dad. She chanted a prayer when the smoke went up, and sang some Indian song.

After that she was calmer. I thought…I don't know what I thought. It was a lame idea." He turns away, his shoulders hunched.

"You thought it would help Fariza if you burned her story." Sid speaks slowly. He wants to make sure he understands correctly. He hates to admit it, but he can almost see Wain's point. Megan used to say, *Put it in a bubble and watch it float away.* This isn't much different, although it has a New Age craziness to it that Sid doesn't like.

Wain nods. "I was imagining I was, like, a shaman, or something. On an island in the wilderness. I thought it would help her like it helped Devi."

Sid smooths the papers in his hands. "I can see that."

"You can?"

"Kinda."

Wain leans into him and Sid doesn't move away. "I didn't mean to make it worse," Wain says. "Is she really upset?"

"Yup," Sid says. "But I'll give her back the pages, tell her you were trying to help. Or you could tell her yourself. Think you can do that?"

Wain nods. "I guess. I'll try anyway."

"Good luck explaining the shaman thing." Sid gets up and starts to walk back to the beach where the boats are. Wain follows him, shuffling across the stones. "Maybe we could have a little ceremony in the backyard or something—that might work," Sid says. "Tell her it's an island thing—that we all write our nightmares down and then burn them. Watch the fear blow away."

Wain turns to face Sid. "Would you do that?"

Sid thinks for a moment. "Yeah," he says. "I could do that. If you tell her you took the pages."

They make their way back to the wharf in silence, Sid in the rowboat, Wain in the kayak. Sid helps Wain haul the kayak up onto the wharf. Nobody seems to have noticed it was gone.

"You've got a golden horseshoe up your ass, don't you?" Sid says.

"What?"

"First the rowboat in Oak Bay. Now this kayak. You got away with stealing—twice."

"You gonna tell?" Wain asks.

Sid shrugs. "Probably not. Least of our worries, right?"

"Yeah." Wain shuffles down the wharf behind Sid. "You were the lucky one, you know."

"Lucky?"

"Yeah—to be brought up here. By Megan and Caleb."

"I know."

"Do you miss her? Devi?"

"No. I hardly remember her."

"I think she misses you."

Sid stops walking and Wain bumps into his back. "Why would you think that?" Sid asks. "She hasn't seen me for fourteen years. She left me here."

"She draws you."

"What do you mean—she draws me? She doesn't know what I look like."

"She has a whole sketchbook full of drawings of white kids: babies and toddlers and little boys. All with eyes like ours. All with ringlets. They're sure as hell not me."

Sid doesn't know what to say. It freaks him out. All those years, Devi was thinking about him, wondering what he looked like. But as far as he knows, she never tried to take him back. She let Megan and Caleb become his parents. Does that make her a good mother or a bad one?

"She's not a bad mother," Wain says, as if reading Sid's mind. "Not really. I mean, I know she loves me, but she's not—you know—reliable. One day she's putting little notes in my school lunch and going to work at the gallery, the next day she won't get out of bed or she goes to a bar and brings home some random guy. When she's manic, she can go for days without sleeping. When she's depressed I have to get Phil or Elizabeth to buy groceries and shit. It's hard."

"I'm sorry," Sid says. "Maybe it'll be better now—Elizabeth says they've got her on lithium. That helps, right?"

"Lithium." Wain spits the word out like a ball of phlegm. "Like that'll last. The side effects are brutal. She never stays on it."

"Oh."

They walk side by side up to the house. Elizabeth's car is parked in the driveway. "Megan said I could stay," Wain says as he trudges up the steps, "but Elizabeth won't let me."

"I know," Sid says. "Maybe you could come back though. Once your mom is feeling better."

"Yeah." Wain pauses on the top step. "Or maybe you could come with me."

"Come with you?"

"To meet Mom. Maybe it would help her."

Before Sid can reply, Elizabeth opens the door and throws her arms around Wain. "It's okay, Nana," he says. "It's okay. Sid found me."

"Thank you, Sid," Elizabeth says. "We're sorry to be so much trouble, aren't we, Wain?"

"Yeah, sorry, Sid," Wain mumbles.

"Run along and pack," Elizabeth says. "The ferry leaves at three."

Sid puts his hand out to stop Wain from going inside. "Um, Elizabeth," he says. "I have an idea. I mean Wain and I had an idea. If you can wait until tomorrow morning to go, then I'll come with you."

"You will?" Wain says.

"Yeah—on one condition."

"What's that?" Elizabeth asks.

"That Chloe comes with me." Sid pauses a moment and then adds, "And Wain promises not to run away again. Oh, and no one pressures us to stay longer than we want to."

"That's three conditions," Elizabeth points out, "but all reasonable, I suppose." She looks slowly from Sid to Wain and back again. "I could call Phil, tell him we're coming tomorrow. He did say that Devi was still"—she searches for the right word—"disoriented."

"She means so doped-up she won't recognize me, let alone you," Wain says.

"Shush, Wain," Elizabeth says. "There's no need for that. Phil says she's getting more lucid by the hour."

"So can we stay, Nana? Please?"

Elizabeth nods. "First ferry tomorrow though. No sleeping in." Wain whoops, picks her up as if she is a child and hops around the porch with her in his arms. She keeps saying, "Put me down, put me down," but she is smiling as she says it.

"I'll go talk to Megan," Sid says. "Make sure it's okay with her. And, Wain, you need to talk to Fariza about that thing."

Wain puts Elizabeth down. "I'm on it, bro," he says.

"What thing?" Elizabeth runs a hand over her hair and smoothes down her shirt where Wain's bear hug has wrinkled it.

"Just something we need to do tonight. But first I need to talk to Chloe. See if she's up for a road trip."

Now You Know

After dinner everyone but Wain and Fariza gathers on the back porch to wait for the sun to go down. Sid has explained the plan to Elizabeth, Chloe and Megan. They have all agreed to write something down to burn in the fire pit Sid has made on the beach. Megan has picked some lavender from her garden to make the smoke smell sweet. One thermos has been filled with coffee, another with hot chocolate. At Chloe's request, Sid has gathered the ingredients for s'mores, although he thinks it might be weird to roast marshmallows over the ashes of their broken dreams. Or it might be exactly right. Time will tell.

Wain is sitting in the dining room with Fariza, who is picking up the balls of crumpled paper he throws on the floor and putting them in the waste basket. Writing down his fears is obviously harder than Wain had anticipated.

Sid isn't sure what Wain said to Fariza, but she seems okay. A bit subdued but okay. Which is pretty much how he feels too. His contribution to the ceremony will be the last six pages of the final Billy saga. And he still has Fariza's pages in his pocket for later.

When Wain and Fariza finally join them, Wain is clutching a single sheet torn from a lined yellow pad. There is writing on both sides. As everyone watches, he folds the paper into an origami lotus and hands it to Fariza, who looks at him as if he has just pulled a live chicken out of his ear. Astonished but intrigued.

"Origami?" Sid says. "You do origami?"

Wain looks at his feet and mutters, "Yeah, I know. Devi taught me a long time ago. Pretty weird, right?"

"Really weird," Sid says. "But very cool." He wonders what other surprises Wain has in store for him. Crocheting? Playing the mandolin? It seems anything is possible.

"Do mine," Chloe says, handing Wain a sheet of pink paper, which he transforms into a perfect lily. Soon the picnic table is littered with origami frogs, boats, birds, bugs, dogs and cats. Only Fariza's pages, which Sid has returned to her, are left unchanged. She clutches the papers in one hand and Fred in the other as they make their way to the beach.

Sid has laid the fire pit with twists of newspaper topped with bits of kindling and stalks of lavendar. He has pulled logs into a semicircle around the pit. There is no wind and the stars are so bright there is no need for flashlights.

He lights a match. "Ready?" he says. Everyone nods. "We're doing this in order of age," he reminds them. "Oldest to youngest." He touches the match to the paper and watches as the flames lick the kindling. When the fire is burning well, Elizabeth steps forward and puts her two little origami frogs into the flames. One for Devi, one for Wain, Sid imagines. Megan's paper dog is next, her pain invisible and unfathomable to Sid. Then it is Sid's turn. Wain has transformed Billy's last story into six different objects: a horse, a snake, a flower, a boat, a hat and a bird. One by one, Sid tosses them into the fire. One by one they burst into flame and then are gone. Sid reaches out to touch the smoke rising from the fire. "Goodbye, old friend," he whispers. Chloe starts to cry when her lily ignites, and she clutches Sid's hand. He wants to ask her what she wrote, but that is another thing they all agreed on: no one has to share.

Wain stands up to throw his yellow lotus into the flames. He hesitates, and Sid thinks he is about to unfold the paper and read what's on it, but instead he just says, "This is for my mom," before he consigns the flower to the fire.

Fariza watches the lotus curl up and turn to ash before she gets up and hands one piece of paper to each person around the fire. "You first," she says to Wain.

"You sure?" he says. She nods, and he leans over the fire, letting one corner catch before he allows the whole sheet to drop onto the flames. Page by page, they burn Fariza's story. Sid can see the words being consumed.

He inhales the smoke and enjoys the stinging sensation in his eyes and the relief that tears bring. When Fariza leans in to burn the last sheet of paper, Chloe starts to sing, slightly off-key. "*When you're down and troubled, when you need a helping hand...*" The others take up the tune. Even Wain and Fariza joins in the chorus. "*You've got a friend, don't you know you've got a friend.*"

Fariza crawls into Sid's lap as they watch the embers die. No one suggests making s'mores. Before they douse and bury the fire, Sid transfers Fariza to Megan's lap and scoops up some ashes in a shovel. When they are cool, he goes from one person to the next, dotting their foreheads with ash. When he is done, Chloe puts her finger in the ashes and touches it gently to his forehead. Even after she wipes her hand on her jeans, he can feel her touch on his forehead: cool, after the heat of the fire.

The next morning, as he eats his cereal, Sid notices that they all still have smudges of ash on their foreheads, himself included. It looks pretty funny, but he knows why he hasn't washed his off. In fact, he wishes he had thought to put some of the ashes in a jar to take with him to Victoria. A touch-up for himself, for Wain, for Chloe, maybe even for Devi. He has never fully understood the meaning of the word *blessing* until now.

He feels bad about leaving Fariza again, but he has tried to help her understand how brief this trip will be.

The passage of time is so hard to explain. Two sleeps. Two breakfasts. Two bedtime stories. Two baths. He chooses books for Megan to read to her when he's away. He gives her his cell phone number and tells her to call anytime. She seems all right this morning. Not talkative, but then she never really is when there are a lot of people around. He wonders if she was always like this, like him. Happier one-on-one. Anxious in a crowd.

"Don't worry about the dishes," Megan says. "Fariza and I will clean up. You got everything you need?" she asks Sid.

"I think so," he says. "Change of clothes, clean underwear, toothbrush, iPod."

"And you'll call when you get there?"

"Sure, Mom," Sid says. Megan's eyes widen. He never calls her Mom, always Megan. "We'll be back before you know it."

"And please tell Irena how sorry I am to have missed her roast beef dinner," Elizabeth says. "I meant to get over to see her before I left, but—"

"My dumb-ass grandson messed up again," Wain chimes in. "Make that my dumb-ass *black* grandson, just so she knows it wasn't her dumb-ass *white* grandson." He grins at Sid. "Tell her I'm sorry too, okay?"

"Okay," Megan says. "Now shoo! You don't want to miss the ferry."

Chloe is sitting at the end of her driveway on an enormous red suitcase. "Two days, Chloe. We're going for two days." Sid groans as he gets out of the car to wrestle the monster into the trunk. He is surprised by how light the suitcase is.

Chloe slams the trunk and hops into the backseat beside him. "Shopping, my friend. Two days of shopping. The suitcase is for the stuff I'll be buying. Deal with it." She leans her head back and sighs. "It's gonna be awesome. And don't look so horrified. You don't have to come."

She puts her head on his shoulder as the car rolls onto the ferry. Before they leave the dock, Sid goes to stand at the rail and look up at his house. He imagines Megan and Fariza filling the dishwasher, wiping down the counters, shaking the crumbs off the placemats. Maybe they'll go for a walk; maybe they'll do some weeding. Megan will read to Fariza. Fariza will have a nap. A flash of red appears on the front porch. Fariza and Megan are waving what appears to be a tablecloth. Sid laughs and waves back, although he doubts they can see him. Chloe appears at his side and yells, "Toro, toro, toro," into the breeze. The ferry pulls away from the dock and they go upstairs to the lounge, where Wain and Elizabeth are playing I Spy.

Wain looks at Sid and says, "I spy with my little eye something that begins with F."

Sid says, "Give it up, Wain. Not in the mood."

"What? I was gonna say *friend*. I spy a *friend*."

Wain looks so aggrieved that Sid decides to play along. He looks around the lounge. A couple of latter-day hippies, a boy and a girl, are dozing in the corner, their dog curled up at their feet. "I spy with my little eye something that begins with D," he says.

"Dope?" Chloe asks. "A dog? Doritos?"

Elizabeth joins the game. "Denim? Dreadlocks? The Doobie Brothers?"

"Driftwood? Duck? A dolphin?" Wain points out the window.

Sid laughs. "There's no dolphin." He was going to say *doofus* but it seems too mean now, especially after Wain has said *friend* rather than *fag*.

"Give up?" They nod and he points toward the sleeping hippies. "Dreamers," he says. "I spy dreamers."

Wain snorts and says, "No one would ever guess that. Your turn, Chloe."

They play I Spy until it's time to go down to the car. No one has been able to guess anyone else's word, but it doesn't matter. It passes the time and keeps Sid from thinking about where he's going and what he's doing.

Wain and Chloe are plugged into their iPods, Sid naps and Elizabeth listens to some classical music station as she drives. They only make one stop on the way down the island, to eat the lunch Megan has packed for them and use the bathrooms in a small roadside park.

When they pull into the driveway at Devi's house, Phil comes out of the garage to greet them.

"Good trip?" he asks.

"Exhausting," Elizabeth says. "I need to freshen up before I go to the hospital."

"You're going right now?" Wain asks. "We only just got here."

"I didn't drive like a bat out of hell all the way down the island so I could put my feet up when I got here," Elizabeth replies. "Take your things inside, Wain. We're leaving in ten minutes."

"Can't I go tomorrow?" he asks. "I'm tired."

"So am I," Elizabeth says. "Phil told your mother we'd be there today, so that's what we're doing, tired or not."

"Okay, okay," Wain says. He slouches into the house, his shoulders hunched.

"I guess you're in the loft again, Sid," Phil says. "Or Chloe can have the loft and you can sleep in my bed. Doesn't matter to me. The sheets are clean. I'll stay at Devi's with Wain until she comes home."

"When's that going to be?" Sid asks.

"When she's stabilized. Couple of weeks, maybe more."

Sid nods and starts toward the garage. "You want the loft?" he asks Chloe, who is extricating her suitcase from the trunk.

"Nah," she says. "No way I'm getting this puppy up a ladder." She sets the suitcase on its wheels and follows Sid.

"You gonna go with them?" she says.

"Now? No. Tomorrow. I'll go tomorrow. With you. And only for a few minutes."

"You sure? That you want me there? I mean, I'm nobody to her. And you might want to talk—privately."

"You're not nobody to me. I need you to be there. Not Elizabeth. Not Wain. You. And I doubt whether we're going to talk much. She's all doped up."

"Okay, okay. Just checking. As long as I get time to shop, I'll be happy. I don't suppose Elizabeth knows where someone my age would shop."

"I doubt it, but remember I told you about those girls who helped me look for Wain. Amie and Enid? They'll know where you should go, although they're pretty big into vintage, I think. And I wanted to see them anyway. Tell them what's happening."

"I can do vintage," Chloe says. "Can you call them tonight?"

"Sure," Sid says. He opens the door to the garage.

"Awesome smell," Chloe says as they walk through to the living quarters. "And this apartment is soooo tiny and adorable."

"Wait till you see the bathroom," Sid says. "Devi tiled the shower walls. It's really beautiful but kinda creepy."

He carries his stuff up to the loft and lies down for a moment, staring up at the skylight. He can hear Phil talking to Chloe, showing her around, offering her a drink. He hears Elizabeth's car start up and drive away. The door to the garage opens and shuts. Phil's and

Chloe's voices move farther away, into the garden. A flock of Canada geese flies overhead in perfect formation. Geese are a good omen, he decides, unlike crows. Geese are orderly, purposeful, community-minded birds. Maybe they're flying to Jimmy Chicken Island.

Chloe's giggle floats up from the garden, like a bubble in a glass of soda. Fizzy, funny Chloe. He feels calm, calmer than he thought he'd feel. He knows that tomorrow he might feel differently, but today he's okay. He's here to support his brother and his grandmother. He chose to be here. He's with his best friend. He's going to get the visit with Devi over with and go home. It's that simple, he thinks as he drifts off to sleep.

Over the Moon

P hil takes Sid and Chloe to the hospital after breakfast the next day. Elizabeth is already there; Wain is
at home, asleep.

"Seeing Devi yesterday was hard for Wain," Phil says
as they wait for an orderly to buzz them into the ward.
"She doesn't look so good." He doesn't elaborate, and Sid
imagines her as haggard, wild-haired, filthy. A lunatic,
shackled to her bed.

Any sense of well-being Sid had experienced the
night before evaporates as they approach the psych ward,
which is on the top floor of the hospital. He wishes he
had never agreed to watch *One Flew Over the Cuckoo's
Nest* with Chloe. He grabs Chloe's hand. His mouth is
dry, but his palms are sweaty. He hopes she doesn't mind.

She squeezes his hand and whispers, "It's gonna be okay."

The door swings open to reveal a dingy green corridor that leads to an elevated, glassed-in nurses' station overlooking a lounge full of grungy couches and battered coffee tables. A big-screen TV is tuned to something with an irritating laugh track. *Happy Days.* Half a dozen patients stare blankly at the screen. No one is laughing, not even when Fonzie says, "It's a lot of fun in la-la land." The studio audience shrieks with joy.

Phil stops at the nurses' station and checks in.

"She's doing better today," a young nurse named Sandra says. She is dressed, as are all the nurses, in street clothes: jeans, sneakers, cheerful T-shirts. She smiles at Sid and Chloe. "First time here? Kinda freaky, right? But don't worry. I'm not Nurse Ratched and we don't do lobotomies anymore." Before Sid can recover from the fact that a) she appears to have read his mind and b) she has a really dark sense of humor, she picks up a chart and says, "Devi's a little more alert today. It helps that her family is here. Although we have to make sure she doesn't get overtired."

Phil nods and leads Sid and Chloe down another green corridor, this one lined with patients' rooms. Some of the doors are open and Sid can see the inmates, none of whom look at all like Jack Nicholson. Most of them are dressed in hospital pajamas. They look more defeated than anything else, lying on their hospital beds, staring out the chicken-wired windows. Their rooms are devoid of decoration. Sid hangs back when they get to Devi's room. He feels queasy.

"Let me tell them you're here," Phil says. "Make sure this is an okay time."

Sid tries to smile, but his lips stick to his teeth. It's not an okay time for me, he thinks. He starts to move away down the hall, but Chloe pulls him back. She's strong for a small girl. All those Polish peasant genes.

"What are you doing?" she hisses.

"Leaving," he says.

"No way."

"I don't want to see her. I made a mistake. I need to leave. Now. This isn't going to do me any good."

"You don't know that," Chloe says. "Did it ever occur to you that this wasn't all about you? That it's about Wain and Devi and Elizabeth too?"

"Fuck you," Sid says. "I'm outta here." He yanks his hand away from Chloe just as Phil comes out of the room.

"She's ready," Phil says. He looks from Chloe to Sid. "You okay, Sid?"

"He's fine," Chloe says sweetly. "Aren't you, Sid?" She stands on tiptoe and kisses him softly on the cheek. Then she takes his hand in hers again and they walk together through the open door. Phil closes it behind them and waits in the hall. The room is dim, the only light coming from a high, barred slit of a window. It's a horrible room—depressing, definitely the worst on the ward—but Sid doubts whether someone as doped-up as Devi cares.

Elizabeth is sitting next to the bed, her hands in her lap. Her eyes are fixed on the figure in the bed. Devi is very,

very thin, her body almost child-size under the blankets. Soft gray curls frame a face that is all angles, although her cracked lips are full. A cut on her forehead bears three stitches and one arm is bandaged. An iv drips clear liquid into her other arm. Her fingernails are clean and clipped short, but her hands look chapped and raw.

Chloe steps up to the bed, pulling Sid after her. "I'm Chloe," she says, "and this is Sid. He's a bit freaked out at the moment, but I'm sure he'll stop acting like a total whiny baby pretty soon."

Devi opens her eyes and tries to focus. "Sid," she says.

"He's not always like this," Chloe continues. "Usually he's pretty cool. Not exactly outgoing though, are you, Sid?"

She nudges Sid, who continues to stare silently at Devi. She's so small, he thinks. So helpless. So—he searches for the right word—*fragile*. Like a robin's egg that has dropped from a nest. There is nothing about her that screams *Mother* or *monster*. Nothing at all.

He clears his throat. "I don't know what to say," he croaks.

Devi nods. "Me too." She coughs and Elizabeth hands her a plastic glass of water with a striped bendy straw, the kind Megan keeps for when kids are sick.

"The medication makes her mouth very dry," Elizabeth explains as Devi drinks.

"I'm sorry you're sick," Sid says. "I hope you get better soon." He knows he sounds lame, as if she has the flu or maybe pneumonia—something ordinary and curable—

but his own mouth is dry and his brain has shorted out. He hopes it's temporary.

"Yes," Devi says. Her eyes close and she turns her head away from him.

That's it? Sid thinks. My big reunion? A tiny sick woman in a hospital bed. Three little words. He shakes his head.

"She'll sleep now," Elizabeth says. "I know it's hard for you to understand, but she made a huge effort today. Huge." Her eyes fill with tears as she smoothes the covers over Devi. "You'll come back tomorrow, won't you? I know she wants to see you again."

How can you tell? Sid wonders, although he knows he will return. He has promised Wain they would come together while Chloe goes shopping.

"Yes," he says. "But then we're going home."

A voice from the bed whispers, "Home."

The next day, Sandra greets Wain by name when he and Sid arrive on the ward. Today she is wearing a pink T-shirt that says *I will get my OCD under control…as soon as I wash my hands one more time.*

Wain stares at her chest a long time and then laughs. Sid's pretty sure Wain doesn't need that much time just to read a slogan.

"Not as funny as the one you had on the other day, the paranoid one! I loved that." He turns to Sid. "It was awesome. What did it say again, Sandy?"

"Paranoid? You would be too if everyone was out to get you. The guys love it." Sandy and Wain cackle. An old man watching TV yells, "Sucked in the vacuum cleaner!" and someone else tells him to shut up.

"Business as usual," Sandy says. "You can go on down to your mom's room. She's expecting you. She's much better today. I called your grandmother and told her there was no need to rush in. She said you two were coming. She has a meeting with Devi's team this morning."

"Her team?" Sid asks as he and Wain walk down the hall to Devi's room.

"Shrink, social worker, nutritionist, massage therapist, yoga instructor, priest. Who knows? The Dalai Lama could be on her team for all I know."

"That'd be cool," Sid says.

"I guess." Wain stops outside the door, shuts his eyes and takes a few deep breaths. In through the nose, out through the mouth. Relaxation breathing. Megan taught Sid to use it years ago. Maybe Devi did the same for Wain at some point.

Sid fills his lungs and lets the air out with a *whoosh*. "The Dalai Lama would be proud," he says as they open the door to Devi's room.

Devi is sitting up in bed, eating breakfast. Cream of Wheat, weak tea, orange juice. Gross. The IV has been disconnected, but the pole is lurking in a corner. She pushes the tray away when they come in. When she speaks, her words are a bit slurred.

"My boys," she says. She holds her hand out to Wain, who leans over and kisses her. Sid stays at the end of the bed.

"Thank you for coming, Sid," she says. "You didn't have to."

"Actually, I did. Or Wain would have beaten me up."

Devi laughs. It's a strange sound in the dim room—clear and deep as the water in Sid's favorite lake.

"Is that true, Wain?" she says.

"I could," Wain says. "He's such a—"

"Such a what?" Sid asks, waiting for the words. *Pussy. Faggot.*

"A wimp," Wain says. "He's, like, a pacifist or something."

"That true, Sid?" Devi smiles. Her teeth are perfectly straight but dingy, as if she had orthodontics but never brushed her teeth. "Are you a pacifist? Or a wimp?"

Sid shrugs. "Bit of both, I guess. Depending on the situation."

"Very commendable," Devi says.

"Very stupid," Wain says. He reaches over and punches Sid on the shoulder. Sid ignores him.

"Nana tells me that Sid's"—Devi hesitates—"Sid's mother has invited you to stay with them until school starts." This is the longest sentence she has spoken and she seems exhausted by the effort. Her eyes close and she leans back on the pillows.

"Can I go?" Wain asks.

Devi's eyes remained closed as she says, "Do you want to?"

Wain nods and then realizes she can't see him.

"It's so cool, Mom. There's this tiny island, and Sid took me to this amazing lake. And his dad says he'll teach me how to fish. I'd come home whenever you want. Whenever you're feeling better. For school for sure. I could bring you a salmon. And Irena—that's Chloe's grandmother—makes awesome jam from her own raspberries. I could bring you a jar—"

Devi opens her eyes and holds up her hand. "Stop, stop. I was there too, a long time ago. When Sid was little. I'm sure he doesn't remember."

Sid stays silent. There's no point in telling her she is right. She gazes at Sid, her eyes damp. "You've had a good life," she says. It's not a question.

"The best," Sid says.

"All right then." She pulls herself up in the bed. "Wain, if Sid's okay with it, you can go. Sid? What do you think?"

Sid glances up at the little slit of a window. He can see a scrap of blue sky through the bars. A bird—not a crow, a starling maybe—zips by, intent on...what? Finding food for his family, catching an updraft, romancing a hot starling chick? What *does* he think about Wain coming back with him? He wishes Megan was here to tell him what to do. A few days ago, he was sure it was the worst idea ever. He still thinks his brother is a pain. He realizes the rest of his summer will be crowded and noisy if Wain comes home with him. But the fact remains: Wain's life sucks and his doesn't. There's no way around that.

"Two conditions," he says. "No fighting. No swearing. And oh, yeah, no stealing."

Wain laughs. "See what I mean, Mom? Stupid. That's three conditions, dummy."

"Let's make it four then," Sid says. "No name-calling."

Devi laughs. "Sucks to be you." Sid isn't sure which one of them she is talking to, but for a moment she sounds just like Wain. "Thank you, Sid." She reaches out to take his hand. He hopes his palms aren't sweaty again. "Thank your mother for me," she says. "For everything."

"I will."

"I need to sleep now," Devi says. "Be good, Wain. I mean it."

Her eyes close, and Wain leans over to kiss her cheek. "Get better, Mommy," he whispers. "See you soon."

He turns and walks out the door. Sid stays in the room a moment, watching Devi's face as she surrenders to sleep.

I can walk away, he thinks. I can go home now. I don't have to come back unless I want to. He reaches over and strokes Devi's sunken cheek.

"Be well, Devi," he says.

He straightens up and walks out the door. Wain is waiting in the corridor, wiping his nose on his sleeve.

"Ready to go, asshole?" Wain says.

"Ready as I'll ever be," Sid says.

Acknowledgments

Many thanks to Monique Polak, cheerleader extraordinaire, who read the book in its early stages and provided valuable feedback and much-needed support. Thanks also to the usual suspects for their friendship, laughter, insight and patience: Jennifer Cameron, Lynne Van Luven, Brian and Hatsumi Harvey, Margaux Finlayson, Robin Stevenson, Maggie de Vries, Bruce Collins, Christine Toller, Fiona Harvey, Christian Down, Joan Backus and Yvonne Haist. And of course, endless gratitude to the Orca team for putting heart and soul into every book Orca publishes. Special thanks to Mike Deas for the amazing cover and for sharing his thoughts about the art of comics. I am also grateful for the grant I received from the British Columbia Arts Council to write this book.

Sarah N. Harvey is the author of nine books for children and young adults. Some of her books have been translated into Korean, German and Slovenian, none of which she speaks or reads (although she is trying to learn Italian). Her novel *The Lit Report* has been optioned for a feature film. She will not be in it. Sarah lives and writes in Victoria, British Columbia. Visit www.sarahnharvey.com for more information.